Charles Dickens

Mrs. Lirriper's Legacy

The Extra Christmas Number of all the Year round

Charles Dickens

Mrs. Lirriper's Legacy
The Extra Christmas Number of all the Year round

ISBN/EAN: 9783743444126

Printed in Europe, USA, Canada, Australia, Japan

Cover: Foto ©Andreas Hilbeck / pixelio.de

More available books at **www.hansebooks.com**

M͟R͟S LIRRIPER'S LEGACY,

THE EXTRA CHRISTMAS NUMBER

OF

ALL THE YEAR ROUND,

CONDUCTED BY

CHARLES DICKENS,

FOR CHRISTMAS, 1864.

CONTENTS:

LONDON: 26, WELLINGTON STREET, STRAND, W.C.;
CHAPMAN & HALL. 193, PICCADILLY, W.
AND ALL BOOKSELLERS AND NEWSMEN.

Price Fourpence.

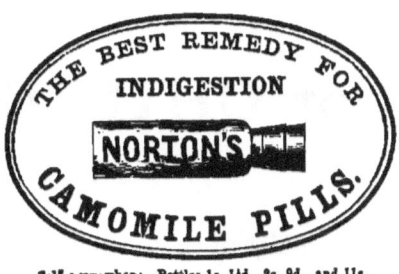

BROWN AND POLSON'S
PATENT CORN FLOUR

WARRANTED PERFECTLY PURE.

IN JELLY

It is quite clear, retains its solidity longer than the best quality of Arrowroot, and is much recommended

For CHILDREN'S DIET.

By the highest class families BROWN & POLSON'S CORN FLOUR has been adopted for excellence of quality, and the numerous purposes to which it is applicable. Being inexpensive and easily prepared, BROWN & POLSON believe that their Corn Flour in its distinctive uses will obtain the patronage of all classes, and soon become

INDISPENSABLE TO EVERY FAMILY.

CORRECTED RECIPE FOR INFANT'S FOOD.

To two teaspoonsful of Brown and Polson's Corn Flour mixed with two table-spoonsful of cold water add half a pint of boiling milk and water (equal quantities), boil for seven minutes, and sweeten very slightly. It should be when warm about the thickness of cream.

TO FAMILIES.

"John Brown," "John Polson," is now signed by the makers upon each packet, as purchasers are sometimes deceived by the substitution of cheap qualities that counterfeit the appearance of Brown and Polson's.

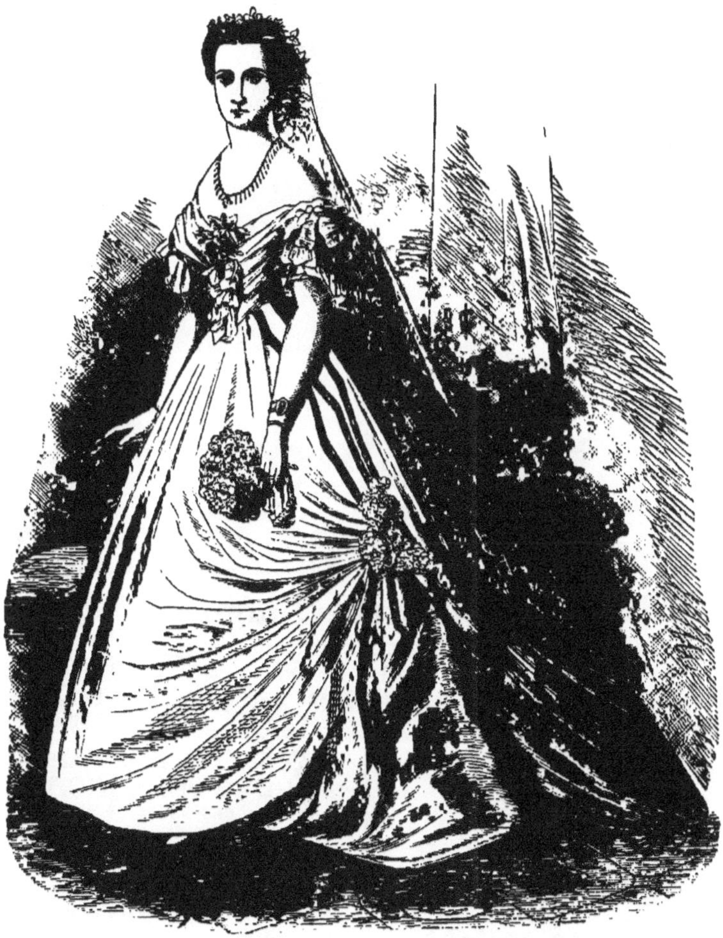

CRINOLINE IN THE DRAWING-ROOM, 1865.

THOMSON'S

"PRIZE MEDAL" SKIRTS,

M^{RS} LIRRIPER'S LEGACY.

THE EXTRA CHRISTMAS NUMBER OF **ALL THE YEAR ROUND.**

CONDUCTED BY CHARLES DICKENS.

CONTAINING THE AMOUNT OF TWO ORDINARY NUMBERS.

CHRISTMAS, 1864.

Price
4d.

I.

MRS. LIRRIPER RELATES
HOW SHE WENT ON, AND WENT OVER.

AH! It's pleasant to drop into my own easy-chair my dear though a little palpitating what with trotting up-stairs and what with trotting down, and why kitchen-stairs should all be corner stairs is for the builders to justify though I do not think they fully understand their trade and never did, else why the sameness and why not more conveniences and fewer draughts and likewise making a practice of laying the plaster on too thick I am well convinced which holds the damp, and as to chimney-pots putting them on by guess-work like hats at a party and no more knowing what their effect will be upon the smoke bless you than I do if so much, except that it will mostly be either to send it down your throat in a straight form or give it a twist before it goes there. And what I says speaking as I find of those new metal chimneys all manner of shapes (there's a row of 'em at Miss Wozenham's lodging-house lower down on the other side of the way) is that they only work your smoke into artificial patterns for you before you swallow it and that I'd quite as soon swallow mine plain, the flavour being the same, not to mention the conceit of putting up signs on the top of your house to show the forms in which you take your smoke into your inside.

Being here before your eyes my dear in my own easy-chair in my own quiet room in my own Lodging House Number Eighty-one Norfolk-street Strand London situated midway between the City and St. James's—if anything is where it used to be with these hotels calling themselves Limited but called Unlimited by Major Jackman rising up everywhere and rising up into flagstaffs where they can't go any higher, but my mind of those monsters is give me a landlord's or landlady's wholesome face when I come off a journey and not a brass plate with an electrified number clicking out of it which it's not in nature can be glad to see me and to which I don't want to be hoisted like molasses at the Docks and left there telegraphing for help with the most ingenious instruments but quite in vain —being here my dear I have no call to mention that I am still in the Lodgings as a business hoping to die in the same and if agreeable to the clergy partly read over at Saint Clement's Danes and concluded in Hatfield churchyard when lying once again by my poor Lirriper ashes to ashes and dust to dust.

Neither should I tell you any news my dear in telling you that the Major is still a fixture in the Parlours quite as much so as the roof of the house, and that Jemmy is of boys the best and brightest and has ever had kept from him the cruel story of his poor pretty young mother Mrs. Edson being deserted in the second floor and dying in my arms, fully believing that I am his born Gran and him an orphan, though what with engineering since he took a taste for it and him and the Major making Locomotives out of parasols broken iron pots and cotton-reels and them absolutely a getting off the line and falling over the table and injuring the passengers almost equal to the originals it really is quite wonderful. And when I says to the Major, "Major can't you by *any* means give us a communication with the guard?" the Major says quite huffy, "No madam it's not to be done," and when I says "Why not?" the Major says, "That is between us who are in the Railway Interest madam and our friend the Right Honourable Vice-President of the Board of Trade" and if you'll believe me my dear the Major wrote to Jemmy at school to consult him on the answer I should have before I could get even that amount of unsatisfactoriness out of the man, the reason being that when we first began with the little model and the working signals beautiful and perfect (being in general as wrong as the real) and when I says laughing "What appointment am I to hold in this undertaking gentlemen?" Jemmy hugs me round the neck and tells me dancing, "You shall be the Public Gran" and consequently they put upon me just as much as ever they like and I sit a growling in my easy-chair.

My dear whether it is that a grown man as clever as the Major cannot give half his heart and mind to anything—even a plaything—but must get into right down earnest with it, whether it is so or whether it is not so I do not undertake to say, but Jemmy is far outdone by the serious and believing ways of the Major in the management of the United Grand Junction Lirriper and Jackman Great Norfolk Parlour Line, "For" says my Jemmy with the sparkling eyes when it was christened, "we must have a whole mouthful of name Gran or our dear old Public" and there the young rogue kissed me, "won't stump up." So the Public took the shares —ten at ninepence, and immediately when that was spent twelve Preference at one-and-sixpence —and they were all signed by Jemmy and countersigned by the Major, and between ourselves much better worth the money than some shares I have paid for in my time. In the same holidays the line was made and worked and opened and ran excursions and had collisions and burst its boilers and all sorts of accidents and offences all most regular correct and pretty. The sense of responsibility entertained by the Major as a military style of station-master my dear starting the down train behind time and ringing one of those little bells that you buy with the little coal-scuttles off the tray round the man's neck in the street did him honour, but noticing the Major of a night when he is writing out his monthly report to Jemmy at school of the state of the Rolling Stock and the Permanent Way and all the rest of it (the whole kept upon the Major's sideboard and dusted with his own hands every morning before varnishing his boots) I notice him as full of thought and care as full can be and frowning in a fearful manner, but indeed the Major does nothing by halves as witness his great delight in going out surveying with Jemmy when he has Jemmy to go with, carrying a chain and a measuring tape and driving I don't know what improvements right through Westminster Abbey and fully believed in the streets to be knocking everything upside down by Act of Parliament. As please Heaven will come to pass when Jemmy takes to that as a profession!

Mentioning my poor Lirriper brings into my head his own youngest brother the Doctor though Doctor of what I am sure it would be hard to say unless Liquor, for neither Physic nor Music nor yet Law does Joshua Lirriper know a morsel of except continually being summoned to the County Court and having orders made upon him which he runs away from, and once was taken in the passage of this very house with an umbrella up and the Major's hat on, giving his name with the door-mat round him as Sir Johnson Jones K.C.B. in spectacles residing at the Horse Guards. On which occasion he had got into the house not a minute before, through the girl letting him on to the mat when he sent in a piece of paper twisted more like one of those spills for lighting candles than a note, offering me the choice between thirty shillings in hand and his brains on the premises marked immediate and waiting for an answer. My dear it gave me such a dreadful turn to think of the brains of my poor dear Lirriper's own flesh and blood flying about the new oilcloth however unworthy to be so assisted, that I went out of my room here to ask him what he would take once for all not to do it for life when I found him in the custody of two gentlemen that I should have judged to be in the feather-bed trade if they had not announced the law, so fluffy were their personal appearance. "Bring your chains sir," says Joshua to the littlest of the two in the biggest hat, "rivet on my fetters!" Imagine my feelings when I pictered him clanking up Norfolk-street in irons and Miss Wozenham looking out of window! "Gentlemen" I says all of a tremble and ready to drop "please to bring him into Major Jackman's apartments." So they brought him into the Parlours, and when the Major spies his own curly-brimmed hat on him which Joshua Lirriper had whipped off its peg in the passage for a military disguise he goes into such a tearing passion that he tips it off his head with his hand and kicks it up to the ceiling with his foot where it grazed long afterwards. "Major" I says "be cool and advise me what to do with Joshua my dead and gone Lirriper's own youngest brother." "Madam" says the Major " my advice is that you board and lodge him in a Powder Mill, with a handsome gratuity to the proprietor when exploded." "Major" I says "as a Christian you cannot mean your words." "Madam" says the Major "by the Lord I do!" and indeed the Major besides being with all his merits a very passionate man for his size had a bad opinion of Joshua on account of former troubles even unattended by liberties taken with his apparel. When Joshua Lirriper hears this conversation betwixt us he turns upon the littlest one with the biggest hat and says "Come sir! Remove me to my vile dungeon. Where is my mouldy straw!" My dear at the picter of him rising in my mind dressed almost entirely in padlocks like Baron Trenck in Jemmy's book I was so overcome that I burst into tears and I says to the Major, "Major take my keys and settle with these gentlemen or I shall never know a happy minute more," which was done several times both before and since, but still I must remember that Joshua Lirriper has his good feelings and shows them in being always so troubled in his mind when he cannot wear mourning for his brother. Many a long year have I left off my widow's mourning not being wishful to intrude, but the tender point in Joshua that I cannot help a little yielding to is when he writes "One single sovereign would enable me to wear a decent suit of mourning for my much-loved brother. I vowed at the time of his lamented death that I would ever wear sables in memory of him but Alas how short-sighted is man, How keep that vow when penniless!" It says a good deal for the strength of his feelings that he couldn't have been seven year old when my poor Lirriper died and to have kept to it ever since is highly creditable. But we know there's good in all of us—if we only knew where it was in some of us—and though it was far from delicate in Joshua to work upon the dear child's feelings when first sent to school and write down into Lincolnshire for his pocket-money by return of post and got it, still he is my poor Lirriper's own youngest brother and mightn't have meant not paying his bill at the Salisbury Arms when his affection took him down to stay a fortnight at Hatfield churchyard and might have meant to keep sober but for bad company. Consequently if the Major *had* played on him with the garden-engine which he got privately into his room without my knowing of it, I think that much as I should have regretted it there would have been words betwixt the Major and me. Therefore my dear though he played on Mr. Buffle by mistake being hot in his head, and though it might have been misrepresented down at Wozenham's into not being ready for Mr. Buffle in other respects he being the Assessed Taxes, still I do not so much regret it as perhaps I ought. And whether Joshua Lirriper will yet do well in life I cannot say, but I did hear of his coming out at a Private Theatre in the character of a Bandit without receiving any offers afterwards from the regular managers.

Mentioning Mr. Buffle gives an instance of there being good in persons where good is not expected, for it cannot be denied that Mr. Buffle's manners when engaged in his business were not agreeable. To collect is one thing and to look about as if suspicious of the goods being gradually removing in the dead of the night by a back door is another, over taxing you have no control but suspecting is voluntary. Allowances too must ever be made for a gentleman of the Major's warmth not relishing being spoke to with a pen in the mouth, and while I do not know that it is more irritable to my own feelings to have a low-crowned hat with a broad brim kept on in-doors than any other hat still I can appreciate the Major's, besides which without bearing malice or vengeance the Major is a man that scores up arrears as his habit always was with Joshua Lirriper. So at last my dear the Major lay in wait for Mr. Buffle and it worrited me a good deal. Mr. Buffle gives his rap of two sharp knocks one day and the Major bounces to the door. "Collector has called for two quarters' Assessed Taxes" says Mr. Buffle. "They are ready for him" says the Major and brings him in here. But on the way Mr. Buffle looks about him in his usual suspicious manner and the Major fires and asks him "Do you see a Ghost sir?" "No sir" says Mr. Buffle. "Because I have before noticed you" says the Major "apparently looking for a spectre very hard beneath the roof of my respected friend. When you find that supernatural agent, be so good as point him out sir." Mr. Buffle stares at the Major and then nods at me. "Mrs. Lirriper sir" says the Major going off into a perfect steam and introducing me with his hand. "Pleasure of knowing her" says Mr. Buffle.

"A—hum!—Jemmy Jackman sir!" says the Major introducing himself. "Honour of knowing you by sight" says Mr. Buffle. "Jemmy Jackman sir" says the Major wagging his head sideways in a sort of an obstinate fury "presents to you his esteemed friend that lady Mrs. Emma Lirriper of Eighty-one Norfolk-street Strand London in the County of Middlesex in the United Kingdom of Great Britain and Ireland. Upon which occasion sir," says the Major, "Jemmy Jackman takes your hat off." Mr. Buffle looks at his hat where the Major drops it on the floor, and he picks it up and puts it on again. "Sir" says the Major very red and looking him full in the face "there are two quarters of the Gallantry Taxes due and the Collector has called." Upon which if you can believe my words my dear the Major drops Mr. Buffle's hat off again. "This—" Mr. Buffle begins very angry with his pen in his mouth, when the Major steaming more and more says "Take your bit out sir! Or by the whole infernal system of Taxation of this country and every individual figure in the National Debt, I'll get upon your back and ride you like a horse!" which it's my belief he would have done and even actually jerking his neat little legs ready for a spring as it was. "This" says Mr. Buffle without his pen "is an assault and I'll have the law of you." "Sir" replies the Major "if you are a man of honour, your Collector of whatever may be due on the Honourable Assessment by applying to Major Jackman at The Parlours Mrs. Lirriper's Lodgings, may obtain what he wants in full at any moment."

When the Major glared at Mr. Buffle with those meaning words my dear I literally gasped for a teaspoonful of sal volatile in a wine-glass of water, and I says "Pray let it go no further gentlemen I beg and beseech of you!" But the Major could be got to do nothing else but snort long after Mr. Buffle was gone, and the effect it had upon my whole mass of blood when on the next day of Mr. Buffle's rounds the Major spruced himself up and went humming a tune up and down the street with one eye almost obliterated by his hat there are not expressions in Johnson's Dictionary to state. But I safely put the street door on the jar and got behind the Major's blinds with my shawl on and my mind made up the moment I saw danger to rush out screeching till my voice failed me and catch the Major round the neck till my strength went and have all parties bound. I had not been behind the blinds a quarter of an hour when I saw Mr. Buffle approaching with his Collecting-books in his hand. The Major likewise saw him approaching and hummed louder and himself approached. They met before the Airy railings. The Major takes off his hat at arm's length and says "Mr. Buffle I believe?" Mr. Buffle takes off *his* hat at arm's length and says "That is my name sir." Says the Major "Have you any commands for me, Mr. Buffle?" Says Mr. Buffle "Not any sir." Then my dear both of 'em bowed very low and haughty and parted, and whenever Mr. Buffle made his rounds in future him and the Major always met and bowed before the Airy railings, putting me much in mind of Hamlet and the other gentleman in mourning before killing one another, though I could have wished the other gentleman had done it fairer and even if less polite no poison.

Mr. Buffle's family were not liked in this neighbourhood, for when you are a householder my dear you'll find it does not come by nature to like the Assessed, and it was considered besides that a one-horse pheayton ought not to have elevated Mrs. Buffle to that heighth especially when purloined from the Taxes which I myself did consider uncharitable. But they were *not* liked and there was that domestic unhappiness in the family in consequence of their both being very hard with Miss Buffle and one another on account of Miss Buffle's favouring Mr. Buffle's articled young gentleman, that it *was* whispered that Miss Buffle would go either into a consumption or a convent she being so very thin and off her appetite and two close-shaved gentlemen with white bands round their necks peeping round the corner whenever she went out in waistcoats resembling black pinafores. So things stood towards Mr. Buffle when one night I was woke by a frightful noise and a smell of burning, and going to my bedroom window saw the whole street in a glow. Fortunately we had two sets empty just then and before I could hurry on some clothes I heard the Major hammering at the attics' doors and calling out "Dress yourselves!—Fire! Don't be frightened!—Fire! Collect your presence of mind!—Fire! All right—Fire!" most tremenjously. As I opened my bedroom door the Major came tumbling in over himself and me and caught me in his arms. "Major" I says breathless "where is it?" "I don't know dearest madam" says the Major—"Fire! Jemmy Jackman will defend you to the last drop of his blood!—Fire! If the dear boy was at home what a treat this would be for him—Fire!" and altogether very collected and bold except that he couldn't say a single sentence without shaking me to the very centre with roaring Fire. We ran down to the drawing-room and put our heads out of window, and the Major calls to an unfeeling young monkey scampering by be joyful and ready to split "Where is it?—Fire!" The monkey answers without stopping "Oh here's a lark! Old Buffle's been setting his house alight to prevent its being found out that he boned the Taxes. Hurrah! Fire!" And then the sparks came flying up and the smoke came pouring down and the crackling of flames and spatting of water and banging of engines and hacking of axes and breaking of glass and knocking at doors and the shouting and crying and hurrying and the heat and altogether gave me a dreadful palpitation. "Don't be frightened dearest madam," says the Major, "—Fire! There's nothing to be alarmed at—Fire! Don't open the street door till I come back—Fire! I'll go and see if I can be of any service—Fire! You're quite composed and comfortable ain't you?—Fire, Fire, Fire!" It was in vain for me to hold the man and tell him he'd be galloped to death by the engines—pumped to death by his over-exertions—wet-feeted to death by the slop and mess—flattened to death when the roofs fell in—his spirit was up and he went scampering off after the young monkey with all the breath he had and none to spare, and me and the girls huddled together at the parlour windows looking at the dreadful flames above the houses over the way, Mr. Buffle's being round the corner. Presently what should we see but some people running down the street straight to our door, and then the Major directing operations in the busiest way, and then some more people and then—carried in a chair similar to Guy Fawkes —Mr. Buffle in a blanket!

My dear the Major has Mr. Buffle brought up our steps and whisked into the parlour and carted out on the sofy, and then he and all the rest of them without so much as a word burst away again full speed, leaving the impression of a vision except for Mr. Buffle awful in his blanket with his eyes a rolling. In a twinkling they all burst back again with Mrs. Buffle in another blanket, which whisked in and carted out on the sofy they all burst off again and all burst back again with Miss Buffle in another blanket, which again whisked in and carted out they all burst off again and all burst back again with Mr. Buffle's articled young gentleman in another blanket—him a holding round the necks of two men carrying him by the legs, similar to the picter of the disgraceful creetur who has lost the fight (but where the chair I do not know) and his hair having the appearance of newly played upon. When all four of a row, the Major rubs his hands and whispers me with what little hoarseness he can get together, "If our dear remarkable boy was only at home what a delightful treat this would be for him!"

My dear we made them some hot tea and toast and some hot brandy-and-water with a little comfortable nutmeg in it, and at first they were scared and low in their spirits but being fully insured got sociable. And the first use Mr. Buffle made of his tongue was to call the Major his Preserver and his best of friends and to say "My for ever dearest sir let me make you known to Mrs. Buffle" which also addressed him as her Preserver and her best of friends and was fully as cordial as the blanket would admit of. Also Miss Buffle. The articled young gentleman's head was a little light and he sat a moaning "Robina is reduced to cinders, Robina is reduced to cinders!" Which went more to the heart on account of his having got wrapped in his blanket as if he was looking out of a violin-cellor-case, until Mr. Buffle says "Robina speak to him!" Miss Buffle says "Dear George!" and but for the Major's pouring down brandy-and-water on the instant which caused a catching in his throat owing to the nutmeg and a violent fit of coughing it might have proved too much for his strength. When the articled young gentleman got the better of it Mr. Buffle leaned up against Mrs. Buffle being two bundles, a little while in confidence, and then says with tears in his eyes which the Major noticing wiped, "We have not been an united family, let us after this danger become so, take her George."

The young gentleman could not put his arm out far to do it, but his spoken expressions were very beautiful though of a wandering class. And I do not know that I ever had a much pleasanter meal than the breakfast we took together after we had all dozed, when Miss Buffle made tea very sweetly in quite the Roman style as depicted formerly at Covent Garden Theatre and when the whole family was most agreeable, as they have ever proved since that night when the Major stood at the foot of the Fire-Escape and claimed them as they came down—the young gentleman headforemost, which accounts. And though I do not say that we should be less liable to think ill of one another if strictly limited to blankets, still I do say that we might most of us come to a better understanding if we kept one another less at a distance.

Why there's Wozenham's lower down on the other side of the street. I had a feeling of much soreness several years respecting what I must still ever call Miss Wozenham's systematic underbidding and the likeness of the house in Bradshaw having far too many windows and a most umbrageous and outrageous Oak which never yet was seen in Norfolk-street nor yet a carriage and four at Wozenham's door, which it would have been far more to Bradshaw's credit to have drawn a cab. This frame of mind continued bitter down to the very afternoon in January last when one of my girls, Sally Rairyganoo which I still suspect of Irish extraction though family represented Cambridge, else why abscond with a bricklayer of the Limerick persuasion and be married in pattens not waiting till his black eye was decently got round with all the company fourteen in number and one horse fighting outside on the roof of the vehicle—I repeat my dear my ill-regulated state of mind towards Miss Wozenham continued down to the very afternoon of January last past when Sally Rairyganoo came banging (I can use no milder expression) into my room with a jump which may be Cambridge and may not, and said "Hurroo Missis! Miss Wozenham's sold up!" My dear when I had it thrown in my face and conscience that the girl Sally had reason to think I could be glad of the ruin of a fellow-creeter, I burst into tears and dropped back in my chair and I says "I am ashamed of myself!"

Well! I tried to settle to my tea but I could not do it with thinking of Miss Wozenham and her distresses. It was a wretched night and I went up to a front window and looked over at Wozenham's and as well as I could make it out down the street in the fog it was the dismalest of the dismal and not a light to be seen. So at last I says to myself "This will not do," and I puts on my oldest bonnet and shawl not wishing Miss Wozenham to be reminded of my best at such a time, and lo and behold you I goes over to Wozenham's and knocks. "Miss Wozenham at home?" I says turning my head when I heard the door go. And then I saw it was Miss Wozenham herself who had opened it and sadly worn she was poor thing and her eyes all swelled and swelled with crying. "Miss Wozenham" I says "it is several years since

there was a little unpleasantness betwixt us on the subject of my grandson's cap being down your Airy. I have overlooked it and I hope you have done the same." "Yes Mrs. Lirriper" she says in a surprise "I have." "Then my dear" I says "I should be glad to come in and speak a word to you." Upon my calling her my dear Miss Wozenham breaks out a crying most pitiful, and a not unfeeling elderly person that might have been better shaved in a nightcap with a hat over it offering a polite apology for the mumps having worked themselves into his constitution, and also for sending home to his wife on the bellows which was in his hand as a writing-desk, looks out of the back parlour and says "The lady wants a word of comfort" and goes in again. So I was able to say quite natural "Wants a word of comfort does she sir? Then please the pigs she shall have it!" And Miss Wozenham and me we go into the front room with a wretched light that seemed to have been crying too and was sputtering out, and I says "Now my dear, tell me all," and she wrings her hands and says "Oh Mrs. Lirriper that man is in possession here, and I have not a friend in the world who is able to help me with a shilling."

It doesn't signify a bit what a talkative old body like me said to Miss Wozenham when she said that, and so I'll tell you instead my dear that I'd have given thirty shillings to have taken her over to tea, only 1 durstn't on account of the Major. Not you see but what I knew I could draw the Major out like thread and wind him round my finger on most subjects and perhaps even on that if I was to set myself to it, but him and me had so often belied Miss Wozenham to one another that I was shamefaced, and I knew she had offended his pride and never mine, and likewise I felt timid that that Rairyganoo girl might make things awkward. So I says "My dear if you could give me a cup of tea to clear my muddle of a head I should better understand your affairs." And we had the tea and the affairs too and after all it was but forty pound, and——There! she's as industrious and straight a creeter as ever lived and has paid back half of it already, and where's the use of saying more, particularly when it ain't the point? For the point is that when she was a kissing my hands and holding them in hers and kissing them again and blessing blessing blessing, I cheered up at last and I says "Why what a waddling old goose I have been my dear to take you for something so very different!" "Ah but I too" says she "how have I mistaken you!" "Come for goodness' sake tell me" I says "what you thought of me?" "Oh" says she "I thought you had no feeling for such a hard hand-to-mouth life as mine, and were rolling in affluence." I says shaking my sides (and very glad to do it for I had been a choking quite long enough) "Only look at my figure my dear and give me your opinion whether if I was in affluence I should be likely to roll in it!" That did it! We got as merry as grigs (whatever they are, if you happen to know my dear—I don't) and I went home to my blessed home as happy and as thankful as could be. But before

I make an end of it, think even of my having misunderstood the Major! Yes! For next forenoon the Major came into my little room with his brushed hat in his hand and he begins "My dearest madam——" and then put his face in his hat as if he had just come into church. As I sat all in a maze he came out of his hat and began again. "My esteemed and beloved friend——" and then went into his hat again. "Major," I cries out frightened "has anything happened to our darling boy?" "No, no, no" says the Major "but Miss Wozenham has been here this morning to make her excuses to me, and by the Lord I can't get over what she told me." "Hoity toity, Major," I says "you don't know yet that I was afraid of you last night and didn't think half as well of you as I ought! So come out of church Major and forgive me like a dear old friend and I'll never do so any more." And I leave you to judge my dear whether I ever did or will. And how affecting to think of Miss Wozenham out of her small income and her losses doing so much for her poor old father, and keeping a brother that had had the misfortune to soften his brain against the hard mathematics as neat as a new pin in the three back represented to lodgers as a lumber-room and consuming a whole shoulder of mutton whenever provided!

And now my dear I really am a going to tell you about my Legacy if you're inclined to favour me with your attention, and I did fully intend to have come straight to it only one thing does so bring up another. It was the month of June and the day before Midsummer Day when my girl Winifred Madgers—she was what is termed a Plymouth Sister, and the Plymouth Brother that made away with her was quite right, for a tidier young woman for a wife never came into a house and afterwards called with the beautifullest Plymouth Twins — it was the day before Midsummer Day when Winifred Madgers comes and says to me "A gentleman from the Consul's wishes particular to speak to Mrs. Lirriper." If you'll believe me my dear the Consols at the bank where I have a little matter for Jemmy got into my head, and I says "Good gracious I hope he ain't had any dreadful fall!" Says Winifred "He don't look as if he had ma'am." And I says "Show him in."

The gentleman came in dark and with his hair cropped what I should consider too close, and he says very polite "Madame Lirrwiper!" I says "Yes sir. Take a chair." "I come," says he "frrwom the Frrwench Consul's." So I saw at once that it wasn't the Bank of England. "We have rrweceived," says the gentleman turning his r's very curious and skilful, "frrwom the Mairrwie at Sens, a communication which I will have the honour to rrwead. Madame Lirrwiper understands Frrwench?" "Oh dear no sir!" says I. "Madame Lirriper don't understand anything of the sort." "It matters not," says the gentleman, "I will trrwanslate."

With that my dear the gentleman after reading something about a Department and a Mairie (which Lord forgive me I supposed till the Major came home was Mary, and never was I more puzzled than to think how that young woman came to have so much to do with it) translated a lot with the most obliging pains, and it came to this :—That in the town of Sens in France, an unknown Englishman lay a dying. That he was speechless and without motion. That in his lodging there was a gold watch and a purse containing such and such money and a trunk containing such and such clothes, but no passport and no papers, except that on his table was a pack of cards and that he had written in pencil on the back of the ace of hearts: "To the authorities. When I am dead, pray send what is left, as a last Legacy, to Mrs. Lirriper Eighty-one Norfolk-street Strand London." When the gentleman had explained all this, which seemed to be drawn up much more methodical than I should have given the French credit for, not at that time knowing the nation, he put the document into my hand. And much the wiser I was for that you may be sure, except that it had the look of being made out upon grocery-paper and was stamped all over with eagles.

"Does Madame Lirrwiper" says the gentleman "believe she rrwecognises her unfortunate compatrrwiot?"

You may imagine the flurry it put me into my dear to be talked to about my compatriots.

I says "Excuse me. Would you have the kindness sir to make your language as simple as you can?"

"This Englishman unhappy, at the point of death. This compatrrwiot afflicted," says the gentleman.

"Thank you sir" I says "I understand you now. No sir I have not the least idea who this can be."

"Has Madame Lirrwiper no son, no nephew, no godson, no frrwiend, no acquaintance of any kind in Frrwance?"

"To my certain knowledge" says I "no relation or friend, and to the best of my belief no acquaintance."

"Pardon me. You take Locataires?" says the gentleman.

My dear fully believing he was offering me something with his obliging foreign manners—snuff for anything I knew—I gave a little bend of my head and I says if you'll credit it, "No I thank you. I have not contracted the habit."

The gentleman looks perplexed and says "Lodgers?"

"Oh!" says I laughing. "Bless the man! Why yes to be sure!"

"May it not be a former lodger?" says the gentleman. "Some lodger that you pardoned some rrwent? You have pardoned lodgers some rrwent?"

"Hem! It has happened sir" says I, "but I assure you I can call to mind no gentleman of that description that this is at all likely to be."

In short my dear we could make nothing of it, and the gentleman noted down what I said and went away. But he left me the paper of which he had two with him, and when the Major came in I says to the Major as I put it in his hand

"Major here's Old Moore's Almanack with the hieroglyphic complete, for your opinion."

It took the Major a little longer to read than I should have thought, judging from the copious flow with which he seemed to be gifted when attacking the organ-men, but at last he got through it and stood a gazing at me in amazement.

"Major" I says "you're paralysed."

"Madam" says the Major, "Jemmy Jackman is doubled up."

Now it did so happen that the Major had been out to get a little information about rail roads and steam-boats, as our boy was coming home for his Midsummer holidays next day and we were going to take him somewhere for a treat and a change. So while the Major stood a gazing it came into my head to say to him "Major I wish you'd go and look at some of your books and maps, and see whereabouts this same town of Sens is in France."

The Major he roused himself and he went into the Parlours and he poked about a little, and he came back to me and he says: "Sens my dearest madam is seventy odd miles south of Paris."

With what I may truly call a desperate effort "Major" I says "we'll go there with our blessed boy!"

If ever the Major was beside himself it was at the thoughts of that journey. All day long he was like the wild man of the woods after meeting with an advertisement in the papers telling him something to his advantage, and early next morning hours before Jemmy could possibly come home he was outside in the street ready to call out to him that we was all a going to France. Young Rosy-cheeks you may believe was as wild as the Major, and they did carry on to that degree that I says "If you two children ain't more orderly I'll pack you both off to bed." And then they fell to cleaning up the Major's telescope to see France with, and went out and bought a leather bag with a snap to hang round Jemmy, and him to carry the money like a little Fortunatus with his purse.

If I hadn't passed my word and raised their hopes, I doubt if I could have gone through with the undertaking but it was too late to go back now. So on the second day after Midsummer Day we went off by the morning mail. And when we came to the sea which I had never seen but once in my life and that when my poor Lirriper was courting me, the freshness of it and the deepness and the airiness and to think that it had been rolling ever since and that it was always a rolling and so few of us minding, made me feel quite serious. But I felt happy too and so did Jemmy and the Major and not much motion on the whole, though me with a swimming in the head and a sinking but able to take notice that the foreign insides appear to be constructed hollower than the English, leading to much more tremenjous noises when bad sailors.

But my dear the blueness and the lightness and the coloured look of everything and the very sentry-boxes striped and the shining rattling drums and the little soldiers with their waists and tidy gaiters, when we got across to the Continent—it made me feel as if I don't know what—as if the atmosphere had been lifted off me. And as to lunch why bless you if I kept a man-cook and two kitchen-maids I couldn't get it done for twice the money, and no injured young women a glaring at you and grudging you and acknowledging your patronage by wishing that your food might choke you, but so civil and so hot and attentive and every way comfortable except Jemmy pouring wine down his throat by tumblers-full and me expecting to see him drop under the table.

And the way in which Jemmy spoke his French was a real charm. It was often wanted of him, for whenever anybody spoke a syllable to me I says "Noncomprenny, you're very kind but it's no use—Now Jemmy!" and then Jemmy he fires away at 'em lovely, the only thing wanting in Jemmy's French being as it appeared to me that he hardly ever understood a word of what they said to him which made it scarcely of the use it might have been though in other respects a perfect Native, and regarding the Major's fluency I should have been of the opinion judging French by English that there might have been a greater choice of words in the language though still I must admit that if I hadn't known him when he asked a military gentleman in a grey cloak what o'clock it was I should have took him for a Frenchman born.

Before going on to look after my Legacy we were to make one regular day in Paris, and I leave you to judge my dear what a day that was with Jemmy and the Major and the telescope and me and the prowling young man at the inn door (but very civil too) that went along with us to show the sights. All along the railway to Paris Jemmy and the Major had been frightening me to death by stooping down on the platforms at stations to inspect the engines underneath their mechanical stomachs, and by creeping in and out I don't know where all, to find improvements for the United Grand Junction Parlour, but when we got out into the brilliant streets on a bright morning they gave up all their London improvements as a bad job and gave their minds to Paris. Says the prowling young man to me "Will I speak Inglis No?" So I says "If you can young man I shall take it as a favour," but after half an hour of it when I fully believed the man had gone mad and me too I says "Be so good as fall back on your French sir," knowing that then I shouldn't have the agonies of trying to understand him which was a happy release. Not that I lost much more than the rest either, for I generally noticed that when he had described something very long indeed and I says to Jemmy "What does he say Jemmy?" Jemmy says looking at him with vengeance in his eye "He is so jolly indistinct!" and that when he had described it longer all over again and I says to Jemmy "Well Jemmy what's it all about?" Jemmy says "He says the building was repaired in seventeen hundred and four, Gran."

Wherever that prowling young man formed his prowling habits I cannot be expected to know, but the way in which he went round the corner while we had our breakfasts and was there again when we swallowed the last crumb was most marvellous, and just the same at dinner and at night, prowling equally at the theatre and the inn gateway and the shop-doors when we bought a trifle or two and everywhere else but troubled with a tendency to spit. And of Paris I can tell you no more my dear than that it's town and country both in one, and carved stone and long streets of high houses and gardens and fountains and statues and trees and gold, and immensely big soldiers and immensely little soldiers and the pleasantest nurses with the whitest caps a playing at skipping-rope with the bunchiest babies in the flattest caps, and clean tablecloths spread everywhere for dinner and people sitting out of doors smoking and sipping all day long and little plays being acted in the open air for little people and every shop a complete and elegant room, and everybody seeming to play at everything in this world. And as to the sparkling lights my dear after dark, glittering high up and low down and on before and on behind and all round, and the crowd of theatres and the crowd of people and the crowd of all sorts, it's pure enchantment. And pretty well the only thing that grated on me was that whether you pay your fare at the railway or whether you change your money at a money-dealer's or whether you take your ticket at the theatre, the lady or gentleman is caged up (I suppose by Government) behind the strongest iron bars having more of a Zoological appearance than a free country.

Well to be sure when I did after all get my precious bones to bed that night, and my Young Rogue came in to kiss me and asks "What do you think of this lovely lovely Paris, Gran?" I says "Jemmy I feel as if it was beautiful fireworks being let off in my head." And very cool and refreshing the pleasant country was next day when we went on to look after my Legacy, and rested me much and did me a deal of good.

So at length and at last my dear we come to Sens, a pretty little town with a great two-towered cathedral and the rooks flying in and out of the loopholes and another tower atop of one of the towers like a sort of a stone pulpit. In which pulpit with the birds skimming below him if you'll believe me, I saw a speck while I was resting at the inn before dinner which they made signs to me was Jemmy and which really was. I had been a fancying as I sat in the balcony of the hotel that an Angel might light there and call down to the people to be good, but I little thought what Jemmy all unknown to himself was a calling down from that high place to some one in the town.

The pleasantest-situated inn my dear! Right under the two towers, with their shadows a changing upon it all day like a kind of a sundial, and country people driving in and out of the court-yard in carts and hooded cabriolets and such-like, and a market outside in front of the cathedral, and all so quaint and like a picter. The Major and me agreed that whatever came of my Legacy this was the place to stay in for our holiday, and we also agreed that our dear boy had best not be checked in his joy that night by the sight of the Englishman if he was still alive, but that we would go together and alone. For you are to understand that the Major not feeling himself quite equal in his wind to the heighth to which Jemmy had climbed, had come back to me and left him with the Guide.

So after dinner when Jemmy had set off to see the river, the Major went down to the Mairie, and presently came back with a military character in a sword and spurs and a cocked-hat and a yellow shoulder-belt and long tags about him that he must have found inconvenient. And the Major says "The Englishman still lies in the same state dearest madam. This gentleman will conduct us to his lodging." Upon which the military character pulled off his cocked-hat to me, and I took notice that he had shaved his forehead in imitation of Napoleon Bonaparte but not like.

We went out at the court-yard gate and past the great doors of the cathedral and down a narrow High Street where the people were sitting chatting at their shop-doors and the children were at play. The military character went in front and he stopped at a pork-shop with a little statue of a pig sitting up, in the window, and a private door that a donkey was looking out of.

When the donkey saw the military character he came slipping out on the pavement to turn round and then clattered along the passage into a back-yard. So the coast being clear, the Major and me were conducted up the common stair and into the front room on the second, a bare room with a red tiled floor and the outside lattice blinds pulled close to darken it. As the military character opened the blinds I saw the tower where I had seen Jemmy, darkening as the sun got low, and I turned to the bed by the wall and saw the Englishman.

It was some kind of brain fever he had had, and his hair was all gone, and some wetted folded linen lay upon his head. I looked at him very attentive as he lay there all wasted away with his eyes closed, and I says to the Major

" I never saw this face before."

The Major looked at him very attentive too, and he says

" I never saw this face before."

When the Major explained our words to the military character, that gentleman shrugged his shoulders and showed the Major the card on which it was written about the Legacy for me. It had been written with a weak and trembling hand in bed, and I knew no more of the writing than of the face. Neither did the Major.

Though lying there alone, the poor creetur was as well taken care of as could be hoped, and would have been quite unconscious of any one's sitting by him then. I got the Major to say that we were not going away at present and that I would come back to-morrow and watch a bit by the bedside. But I got him to add—and I shook my head hard to make it stronger—"We agree that we never saw this face before."

Our boy was greatly surprised when we told him sitting out in the balcony in the starlight, and he ran over some of those stories of former Lodgers, of the Major's putting down, and asked wasn't it possible that it might be this lodger or that lodger. It was not possible and we went to bed.

In the morning just at breakfast-time the military character came jingling round, and said that the doctor thought from the signs he saw there might be some rally before the end. So I says to the Major and Jemmy, "You two boys go and enjoy yourselves, and I'll take my Prayer-Book and go sit by the bed." So I went, and I sat there some hours, reading a prayer for him poor soul now and then, and it was quite on in the day when he moved his hand.

He had been so still, that the moment he moved I knew of it, and I pulled off my spectacles and laid down my book and rose and looked at him. From moving one hand he began to move both, and then his action was the action of a person groping in the dark. Long after his eyes had opened, there was a film over them and he still felt for his way out into light. But by slow degrees his sight cleared and his hands stopped. He saw the ceiling, he saw the wall, he saw me. As his sight cleared, mine cleared too, and when at last we looked in one another's faces, I started back and I cries passionately:

"O you wicked wicked man! Your sin has found you out!"

For I knew him, the moment life looked out of his eyes, to be Mr. Edson, Jemmy's father who had so cruelly deserted Jemmy's young unmarried mother who had died in my arms, poor tender creetur, and left Jemmy to me.

"You cruel wicked man! You bad black traitor!"

With the little strength he had, he made an attempt to turn over on his wretched face to hide it. His arm dropped out of the bed and his head with it, and there he lay before me crushed in body and in mind. Surely the miserablest sight under the summer sun!

"O blessed Heaven" I says a crying, "teach me what to say to this broken mortal! I am a poor sinful creetur, and the Judgment is not mine."

As I lifted my eyes up to the clear bright sky, I saw the high tower where Jemmy had stood above the birds, seeing that very window; and the last look of that poor pretty young mother when her soul brightened and got free, seemed to shine down from it.

"O man, man, man!" I says, and I went on my knees beside the bed; "if your heart is rent asunder and you are truly penitent for what you did, Our Saviour will have mercy on you yet!"

As I leaned my face against the bed, his feeble hand could just move itself enough to touch me. I hope the touch was penitent. It

tried to hold my dress and keep hold, but the fingers were too weak to close.

I lifted him back upon the pillows, and I says to him:

"Can you hear me?"

He looked yes.

"Do you know me?"

He looked yes, even yet more plainly.

"I am not here alone. The Major is with me. You recollect the Major?"

Yes. That is to say he made out yes, in the same way as before.

"And even the Major and I are not alone. My grandson—his godson—is with us. Do you hear? My grandson."

The fingers made another trial to catch at my sleeve, but could only creep near it and fall.

"Do you know who my grandson is?"

Yes.

"I pitied and loved his lonely mother. When his mother lay a dying I said to her, 'My dear this baby is sent to a childless old woman.' He has been my pride and joy ever since. I love him as dearly as if he had drunk from my breast. Do you ask to see my grandson before you die?"

Yes.

"Show me, when I leave off speaking, if you correctly understand what I say. He has been kept unacquainted with the story of his birth. He has no knowledge of it. No suspicion of it. If I bring him here to the side of this bed, he will suppose you to be a perfect stranger. It is more than I can do, to keep from him the knowledge that there is such wrong and misery in the world; but that it was ever so near him in his innocent cradle, I have kept from him, and I do keep from him, and I ever will keep from him. For his mother's sake, and for his own."

He showed me that he distinctly understood, and the tears fell from his eyes.

"Now rest, and you shall see him."

So I got him a little wine and some brandy and I put things straight about his bed. But I began to be troubled in my mind lest Jemmy and the Major might be too long of coming back. What with this occupation for my thoughts and hands, I didn't hear a foot upon the stairs, and was startled when I saw the Major stopped short in the middle of the room by the eyes of the man upon the bed, and knowing him then, as I had known him a little while ago.

There was anger in the Major's face, and there was horror and repugnance and I don't know what. So I went up to him and I led him to the bedside and when I clasped my hands and lifted of them up, the Major did the like.

"O Lord" I says "Thou knowest what we two saw together of the sufferings and sorrows of that young creetur now with Thee. If this dying man is truly penitent, we two together humbly pray Thee to have mercy on him!"

The Major says "Amen!" and then after a little stop I whispers him, "Dear old friend fetch our beloved boy." And the Major, so clever as to have got to understand it all without being told a word, went away and brought him.

Never never never, shall I forget the fair bright face of our boy when he stood at the foot of the bed, looking at his unknown father. And O so like his dear young mother then!

"Jemmy" I says, "I have found out all about this poor gentleman who is so ill, and he did lodge in the old house once. And as he wants to see all belonging to it, now that he is passing away, I sent for you."

"Ah poor man!" says Jemmy stepping forward and touching one of his hands with great gentleness. "My heart melts for him. Poor, poor, man!"

The eyes that were so soon to close for ever, turned to me, and I was not that strong in the pride of my strength that I could resist them.

"My darling boy, there is a reason in the secret history of this fellow-creetur, lying as the best and worst of us must all lie one day, which I think would ease his spirit in his last hour if you would lay your cheek against his forehead and say 'May God forgive you!'"

"O Gran," says Jemmy with a full heart "I am not worthy!" But he leaned down and did it. Then the faltering fingers made out to catch hold of my sleeve at last, and I believe he was a trying to kiss me when he died.

* * * * *

There my dear! There you have the story of my Legacy in full, and it's worth ten times the trouble I have spent upon it if you are pleased to like it.

You might suppose that it set us against the little French town of Sens, but no we didn't find that. I found myself that I never looked up at the high tower atop of the other tower, but the days came back again when that fair young creetur with her pretty bright hair trusted in me like a mother, and the recollection made the place so peaceful to me as I can't express. And every soul about the hotel down to the pigeons in the court-yard made friends with Jemmy and the Major, and went lumbering away with them on all sorts of expeditions in all sorts of vehicles drawn by rampagious cart-horses—with heads and without—mud for paint and ropes for harness—and every new friend dressed in blue like a butcher, and every new horse standing on his hind legs wanting to devour and consume every other horse, and every man that had a whip to crack crack-crack-crack-crack-cracking it as if it was a schoolboy with his first. As to the Major my dear that man lived the greater part of his time with a little tumbler in one hand and a bottle of small wine in the other, and whenever he saw anybody else with a little tumbler, no matter who it was —the military character with the tags, or the inn servants at their supper in the court-yard, or towns-people chatting on a bench, or country-people a starting home after market—down rushes the Major to clink his glass against their glasses and cry—Hola! Vive Somebody! or Vive Something! as if he was beside himself. And though I could not quite approve of the Major's doing it, still the ways of the world are

the ways of the world varying according to different parts of it, and dancing at all in the open Square with a lady that kept a barber's shop my opinion is that the Major was right to dance his best and to lead off with a power that I did not think was in him, though I was a little uneasy at the Barricading sound of the cries that were set up by the other dancers and the rest of the company, until when I says "What are they ever calling out Jemmy?" Jemmy says "They're calling out Gran, Bravo the Military English! Bravo the Military English!" which was very gratifying to my feelings as a Briton and became the name the Major was known by.

But every evening at a regular time we all three sat out in the balcony of the hotel at the end of the court-yard, looking up at the golden and rosy light as it changed on the great towers, and looking at the shadows of the towers as they changed on all about us ourselves included, and what do you think we did there? My dear if Jemmy hadn't brought some other of those stories of the Major's taking down from the telling of former lodgers at Eighty-one Norfolk-street, and if he didn't bring 'em out with this speech:

"Here you are Gran! Here you are God-father! More of 'em! I'll read. And though you wrote 'em for me, Godfather, I know you won't disapprove of my making 'em over to Gran; will you?"

"No my dear boy," says the Major. "Everything we have is hers, and we are hers."

"Hers ever affectionately and devotedly J. Jackman, and J. Jackman Lirriper," cries the Young Rogue giving me a close hug. "Very well then Godfather. Look here. As Gran is in the Legacy way just now, I shall make these stories a part of Gran's Legacy. I'll leave 'em to her. What do you say Godfather?"

"Hip hip Hurrah!" says the Major.

"Very well then," cries Jemmy all in a bustle. "Vive the Military English! Vive the Lady Lirriper! Vive the Jemmy Jackman Ditto! Vive the Legacy! Now, you look out, Gran. And you look out, Godfather. I'll read! And I'll tell you what I'll do besides. On the last night of our holiday here when we are all packed and going away, I'll top up with something of my own."

"Mind you do sir" says I.

"Don't you be afraid, Gran" cries Young Sparkles. "Now then! I'm going to read. Once, twice, three and away. Open your mouths and shut your eyes, and see what Fortune sends you. All in to begin. Look out Gran. Look out Godfather!"

So in his lively spirits Jemmy began a reading, and he read every evening while we were there, and sometimes we were about it late enough to have a candle burning quite steady out in the balcony in the still air. And so here is the rest of my Legacy my dear that I now hand over to you in this bundle of papers all in the Major's plain round writing. I wish I could hand you the church towers over too, and the pleasant air and the inn yard and the pigeons often coming and perching on the rail by Jemmy and seeming to be critical with their heads on one side, but you'll take as you find.

II.

A PAST LODGER RELATES
A WILD STORY OF A DOCTOR.

I have lived in a common-place way, Major, in common-place times, and should have mighty ltitle to tell of my own life and adventures (if I were put to it) that would be likely to interest any one save myself. But I have a story by me that shall be yours if you please. Of this story I have only to say a very few words. My father had the manuscript of it in his possession as long as I can remember, and he once allowed me, when I began to approach years of discretion, to read it.' It was given to him by a very old friend, whom I dimly remember about our house when I was a boy— a French gentleman of obliging manners, and with a melancholy smile. He fades out of the memory of my youthful days very early, and I chiefly remember him because my father told me that he had received this manuscript from him, and that in parting with it the French gentleman had said: "Ah! few people would believe what went on at that time in France, but here's a specimen. I don't expect you to believe it, mind!"

When the time came for examining my deceased father's papers, this paper turned up among the rest. I put it aside, being immersed in business matters at the time, and only came upon it yesterday, in these very lodgings, in the course of a periodical rummage among a great box of papers from my bankers in the Strand hard by. The periodical rummage came to an end directly, and, with the zest naturally derived from a sense that I ought to be doing something else, I read over every word of the manuscript. It is faded and yellow, as you see; and it is odd, as you shall hear. Thus it goes:

It is pretty well known that as the eighteenth century drew towards its close, and as the moment approached when the mighty change which had been long threatening, was actually about to take place—it is well known, I say, that we Parisians had got into a condition of mind, which was about as bad as bad could be. Luxurious, used up, we had for the most part lost all sense of enjoyment; while as to any feeling of duty—Heaven help us! there was little enough of that. What did we believe of man's responsibility? We were here to enjoy ourselves if we could; if we could not—why, there was a remedy.

It was just one of those states of things which all thinking men were able to see, could not possibly last long. A great shock must be at hand, such men said: a constitution so utterly deranged must pass through some serious attack before it would be likely to get better. That "serious attack" came, and the great French Revolution inaugurated a new condition of affairs. What I have to relate, however, has nothing to do with the revolution, but took place some few years before that great convulsion shook the world, and another era began.

It is not to be supposed that men who held the opinions, and led the lives of the better class of Parisians at that time, were happy. Indeed, a frank open-hearted man, who was tolerably content with the world as he found it, and was able and willing to enjoy himself in it, would have been looked upon with contempt by the more enlightened (and miserable) sort, and would have been regarded as a man deficient alike in intellect and "ton." There were few enough of such, however, and the representatives of the morbid class had it all their own way. Of course among these it was not likely that an agency so well calculated to help them out of their difficulties as suicide should be neglected, and it is not too much to say that the sacrifices offered up at that terrible shrine, were beyond all limits of ordinary proportion. It was such a resource to fall back upon, such a quick way out of the difficulty! Was money short? Was a wife troublesome, or a mistress obdurate? Was there a course of east wind setting in? Were pleasures pleasures no longer, while pain was still pain? Was life, for any reason, not worth having: was it a bore, a penance, a hell upon earth? Here was the remedy at hand—get rid of it. As to what lay beyond—pooh! one must take his chance. Perhaps there was nothing. Perhaps there were the Elysian Fields, with endless earthly gratifications, and sempiternal youth and freshness, to make them enjoyable. "Let us be off with all speed," said the weary ones; "who will help us on our way?"

Helpers were not wanting. There were cunning poisons which would dispose of you in a twinkling, and let you know nothing about it. There were baths and lancets, and anybody could seat himself in a warm bath and open one of his own veins and die with decency. Then there were pistols, beautiful little toys all inlaid with silver and mother-of-pearl, and with your own arms let into the butt, and your coronet, if you happened—which was very likely—to be a marquis. And was there not charcoal? The sleep said to be produced by its fumes was of the soundest —no dreams—no waking. But then you must be sure to stop up all the chinks, or you might happen to inhale a breath of air, and so find yourself back among the east winds and creditors, and the rest of the ills of life, with only a congestion of the head for your pains. All the various modes by which our poor little spark of life may be quenched, were in vogue at that time, but there was one particular method of doing the terrible business which was more fashionable than the rest, and of which it is my special business to treat.

There was a certain handsome street in Paris, and in the Faubourg St. Germain, in which there lived a certain learned and accomplished

Doctor. We will call this learned man, Dr. Bertrand. He was a man of striking and rather agreeable appearance, with a fine portly figure, and a handsome and strikingly intelligent face; his age was somewhere between forty and fifty; but there was one characteristic about his countenance, which every one who came in contact with him must have felt, though not all would have been able to explain what it was that affected them. His eyes were dead. They never changed, and they rarely moved. The rest of his face was as mobile as the faces of other people in the average, but not so with the eyes. They were of a dull leaden colour, and they actually seemed dead: the idea being further carried out by the livid and unwholesome tints of the skin around those organs. Judged from its hues, the skin might have mortified.

Dr. Bertrand, in spite of his dead eyes, was a personage of cheerful, almost gay, manners, and of an unvarying and amazing politeness. Nothing ever put him out. He was also a man surrounded by impenetrable mystery. It was impossible to get at him, or to break down the barriers which his politeness erected around him. Dr. Bertrand had made many discoveries by which the scientific world had profited. He was a rich man, and his pecuniary means had increased lately in a marked degree. The Doctor made no secret of his resources; it was part of his nature to enjoy luxury and splendour, and he lived in both. His house, an hotel of moderate size in the Rue Mauconseil, enclosed in a court-yard of its own, filled with shrubs and flowers, was a model of taste. His dining-room especially was the realised ideal of what such an apartment should be. Pictures, beautiful pictures—not pieces of wall furniture—decorated the walls, and these were lighted up at night in the most artful manner by lamps of enormous power. The floor was padded with the most splendid Persian carpets, the curtains and chairs were of the finest Utrecht velvet, and, in a conservatory outside, always heated to the most luxurious point, a fountain played perpetually: the light trickling of its water making music in the beautiful place.

And well might Dr. Bertrand have so perfect a dining-room in his house. To give dinners was a great part of Dr. Bertrand's business. In certain circles those dinners were highly celebrated, but they were always talked about under the rose. It was whispered that their splendour was fabulous; that the dishes and the wines reached a point of perfection absolutely unknown elsewhere; that the guests were waited upon by servants who knew their business, which is saying much; that they dined seated upon velvet fauteuils, and ate from golden plates; and it was said, moreover, that Dr. Bertrand entered into the spirit of the times, that he was a mighty and experienced chemist, and that it was an understood thing that Dr. Bertrand's guests did not feel life to be all they could wish, and had no desire to survive the night which succeeded their acceptance of his graceful hospitality.

Strange and intolerable imputation! Who could live under it? The Doctor could apparently. For he not only lived but throve and prospered under it.

It was a delicate and dainty way of getting out of the difficulties of life, this provided by Dr. Bertrand. You dined in a style of unwonted luxury, and you enjoyed excellent company, the Doctor himself the very best of company. You felt no uneasiness or pain, for the Doctor knew his business better than that; you went home feeling a little drowsy perhaps, just enough so to make your bed seem delightful; you went off to sleep instantly—the Doctor knew to a minute how to time it all—and you woke up in the Elysian Fields. At least that was where you expected to wake up. That, by-the-by, was the only part of the programme which the Doctor could not make sure of.

Now, there arrived at Dr. Bertrand's house one morning, a letter from a young gentleman named De Clerval, in which an application was made, that the writer might be allowed to partake of the Doctor's hospitality next day. This was the usual form observed, and (as was also usual) a very handsome fee accompanied the letter. A polite answer was returned in due time, enclosing a card of invitation for the following day, and intimating how much the Doctor looked forward to the pleasure of making Monsieur de Clerval's acquaintance.

A dull rainy day at the end of November, was not a day calculated to reconcile to life any one previously disapproving of the same. Everything was dripping. The trees in the Champs Elysées, the eaves of the sentry-boxes, the umbrellas of those who were provided with those luxuries, the hats of those who were not; all were dripping. Indeed, dripping was so entirely a characteristic of the day, that the Doctor, with that fine tact and knowledge of human nature which distinguished him, had, in arranging the evening programme, given orders that the conservatory fountain should be stopped, lest it should affect the spirits of his guests. Dr. Bertrand was always very particular that the spirits of his guests should not be damped.

Alfred de Clerval was something of an exception to the Doctor's usual class of visitors. In his case it was not ennui, nor weariness of life, nor a longing for sensation, that made him one of the Doctor's guests. It was a mixture of pique and vexation, with a real conviction that what he had set his heart upon, as alone capable of bringing him happiness, was out of his reach. He was of a rash impetuous nature, he believed that all his chance of happiness was gone for life, and he determined to quit life. Two great causes ordinarily brought grist to Dr. Bertrand's mill; money troubles, and love troubles. De Clerval's difficulties were of the latter description. He was in a fever of love and jealousy. He was, and had been for some time, the devoted lover of Mademoiselle Thérèse de Farclles: a noted beauty of that day. All had gone smoothly for a time, until a certain Vicomte de Noel, a cousin of the lady's, appeared upon the scene, and Alfred de Clerval becoming jealous, certain unpleasant scenes ensued, and finally a serious quarrel: Mademoiselle de Farelles belonging to that class of persons who are too proud to clear themselves from a false imputation when they might otherwise very easily do so. Throughout, De Clerval had never once seen the Vicomte ; indeed, the principal intercourse between this last and Mademoiselle de Farelles, had been by letter, and it was partly this correspondence which had brought the quarrel about.

When De Clerval entered the salon of Dr. Bertrand where the guests were assembled before dinner, he found himself one of eight or ten persons, all about, like himself, to gather round the Doctor's table, with intentions of a desperate kind. Physiognomically they belonged to all manner of types, some being fat in the face, some thin in the face, some florid in the face, and some very pale in the face. In one respect alone there was a similarity among them ; they *all* wore a sort of fixed impregnable expression which was intended to be, and to a certain extent was, unfathomable.

It has been said that there was every sort of person in this assembly. Here was, for instance, a fat man with a countenance naturally jovial, plethoric, in want of a little doctoring no doubt, too much of a "bon vivant" assuredly, but why on earth here now? If he had come in the morning to consult the Doctor on his digestion, one could understand ; but what does he do here now ? That man knows that to-morrow morning it will be proclaimed to the world that he is ruined, and an impostor. His affairs will collapse, like a house made of cards, and he who has an especial affection for social importance, and who has hitherto enjoyed a good position among his fellows, knows that he would never be able to show his face again. True to his sociability and love of company, to the last, he comes to make an end in good society. Surely no other system, but Dr. Bertrand's, would ever have met the views of this unhappy speculator. Honour then to Dr. Bertrand! who provides every class of persons with the means of suicide.

Here, again, is an individual of another description altogether. A dark thin close-shaved man, who has the fixed unfathomable expression more developed than all the others. This morning his valet knocked at his door, and brought him a letter directed to Monsieur, which the fille de chambre had found on Madame's dressing-table. Madame herself was not in the room, there was only the letter lying before the looking-glass. Monsieur read it, and he is here dining with Dr. Bertrand, and his face is deadly white, and he does not speak a word.

Such guests as these and De Clerval were of an exceptional character. The right man in the right place was a tall faded young man, whom Alfred observed leaning against the chimney-piece, too languid to sit, stand, or recline, and so driven to lean. He had a handsome countenance as far as symmetry of feature and proportion went, but the expression was terrible : so blank, so weary, so hopeless,

that one really almost felt that his coming there to dine with Dr. Bertrand was the best thing he could do. He was splendidly dressed, and the value of his waistcoat buttons and studs, seemed to prove that it was not poverty which had brought him there : just as the utter vapidity and blankness of his weary face seemed to indicate that he was incapable of such a strength of love as would drive him to this last resource. No, this was a case of ennui: hopeless, final, terrible. Some of his friends had dined with Dr. Bertrand, and it seemed to have answered, as they never bored him again. He thought he would try it, so here he was come to dinner. Others were there, like this one. Men who had already outlived themselves, so to speak—outlived their better selves—their belief, their health, their natural human interest in the things that happen beneath the sun—men whose hearts had gone to the grave long ago, and whose bodies were now to follow.

" We do not go through the ceremony of introduction in these little réunions of ours," whispered the Doctor in De Clerval's ear ; "we are all supposed to 'now each other." This was after the servant had solemnly announced dinner, and when the guests and their entertainers were passing to the salle-à-manger.

The room looked charming. The Doctor had not only caused the fountains to be stopped, but had even, to increase the comfort of the scene, directed that the great velvet curtains should be drawn over the entrance to the conservatory. The logs blazed upon the hearth, and the table was covered with glittering candles. For the Doctor well knew the effect of these, and how they add to the gaiety of every scene into which they are introduced.

The guests all took their places round that dreadful board, and perhaps at that moment—always a chilly one, under the circumstances—a serious sense of what they were doing forced itself upon some of them. Certainly Alfred de Clerval shuddered as he sat down to table, and certain good thoughts made a struggle to gain possession of his mind. But the die was cast. He had come to that place with an intent known to everybody present, and he must go through with the intent. He thought, too, that he caught the Doctor's eye fixed upon him. He must be a man—a MAN.

The Doctor seemed a little anxious at about this period of the entertainment, and now and then would sign impatiently to the servants to do their work swiftly. And so the oysters went round, and then some light wine. It was Château Yquem. The Doctor's wine was matchless.

Dr. Bertrand seemed resolved that there should be no pauses in the conversation, and tore himself to tatters—though apparently enjoying himself extremely—in order to keep it going at this time. There was one horrible circumstance connected with the flagging talk. No one alluded to the future. Nobody spoke of to-morrow. It would have been indelicate in the host ; in the guests it would have been folly.

"On such a day as this," remarked the Doctor, addressing a distinguished looking spectre at the other end of the table, "you will have missed your drive in the Bois, M. le Baron?"

"No," replied the person addressed, "I was there in the afternoon for two hours."

"But the fog—could you see?"

"I had runners before me with torches. I had the idea that it might prove interesting."

"And, was it?" inquired another spectral personage, looking up suddenly: as if he rather regretted having committed himself to the Doctor's hospitality before trying this new experiment. "*Was* it interesting?"

"Not in the remotest degree," replied the Baron, in an extinguished sort of voice, and to the other's evident satisfaction. "It was impossible to go beyond a foot-pace, nothing but a grey mist was to be seen on all sides, the horses were bewildered and had to be led. In short, it was an experience to make a man commit sui——"

"Allow me strongly to recommend this salmi," cried the Doctor, in a loud voice. "My chef is particularly good at it." The Baron had got upon an awkward tack, and it was necessary to interrupt him. Dr. Bertrand well knew how difficult it was on these occasions to keep that horrid word, which the Baron had so nearly spoken, out of the conversation. Everybody tried to avoid it, but it would come up.

"For my part, I spent the day at the Louvre," said a little man with a green complexion, and all his features out of drawing. He was a gentleman who had hitherto been entirely unsuccessful in putting an end to himself. He had been twice cut down, and once sewn up when he had had the misfortune to miss his jugular by the eighth of an inch. He had been saved from drowning by a passing friend, whom he hated ever afterwards. He had charcoaled himself, forgetting to stop up the keyhole; and he had jumped out of window, just in time to be caught by a passing manure-cart. "I spent the day at the Louvre," remarked this unfortunate gentleman; "the effect of the fog upon some of the pictures was terrible."

"Dear me!" said the gentleman who had before regretted having missed the Bois in a fog, and who on the whole seemed to have come to the Doctor's prematurely; "I should like to have seen that very much, very much indeed. I wonder if there will be a fog to-to——"

"To-morrow," he was going to say. The Doctor thought the moment a propitious one for sending round the champagne; and even in this assembly it did its usual work, and the buzz of talk followed as it circulated.

"This poulet," said the Doctor, "is a dish on which we pride ourselves rather." It was curious that the Doctor's guests always had a disposition to avoid those dishes which he recommended the most strongly. They knew why they were come, and that was all very well; but there was something treacherous in recommending things. But the Doctor was up to this. He had given enough of these entertainments to enable him to observe how regular this shyness was in its action, and so he thus paved the way for the next dish, which was always *the* dish he wanted his guests to partake of, and which they did partake of almost invariably. The next dish in this case was a new one, a "curry à l'Anglaise," and almost everybody rushed at it headlong. The dish was a novelty even in England then, and in France wholly unknown. The Doctor smiled as he raised the champagne to his lips. "There is a fine tonic quality about these English curries," he remarked.

"And tonics always disagree with my head," said a little man at the end of the table, who had not yet spoken. And he ate no more curry.

Alfred de Clerval was, in spite of his sorrows, so far alive to all that was going on around him as to miss partaking of some of Dr. Bertrand's favourite dishes. He had also entered into conversation with one of his next neighbours. On his left was the commercial man, whose exposure was to take place next day; and this gentleman, naturally a bon vivant, was making the most of his time, and committing fearful havoc on the Doctor's dishes and wine. On the right of De Clerval was a gentleman whom Alfred had not observed until they were seated together at table, but he was a remarkable looking man. They talked at first of indifferent matters, or of what went on around them. They *got on* together, as the saying goes. Men are not very particular in forming acquaintances when their duration is likely to be short, and so when the wine had circulated for some time—and every man there partook of it fiercely—these two had got to speak freely, for men who were but friends of an hour.

"You are a young man," said the stranger, after a pause, during which he had observed De Clerval closely; "you are a young man to be dining with Dr. Bertrand."

"The Doctor's hospitality is, I suspect, suited at times to persons of all ages," replied Alfred. "I was going to add, and of both sexes. How is it, by-the-by, that there are no ladies among the Doctor's guests?"

"I suppose he won't have them," retorted the other, with bitterness; "and he is right! They would be going into hysterics in the middle of dinner, and disorganising the Doctor's arrangements, as they do disorder every system of which they form a part, even to the great world itself."

"True enough," thought Alfred to himself. "This man has suffered as I have, from being fool enough to put his happiness in a woman's keeping."

De Clerval stole a look at him. He was a man considerably his own senior. He was a very tall man, and had something of that languid air in all his movements which often belongs to height. His face was deeply marked for his age, but there was a very kind and merciful expression on it, and, though he looked weary and perhaps indolent, his was not by any means a blasé countenance. He looked like a man who has goodness in him, but instinctively and quite independent of any influence wrought by principle. A good nature, kind generous and honourable, was there; but the man had no rudder or compass to steer by. It was a fine new vessel adrift.

In his own terrible position one would say that such an one could have no leisure to think of anything else. A man under such circumstances might be excused for a little egotism, might be expected to be absorbed in himself and his own troubles; but it was not so with this stranger. His eye wandered from time to time round the table, and evidently his mind was largely occupied with speculations as to what the rest of Dr. Bertrand's patients were suffering under. "How curious it would be," he at length remarked to De Clerval, "if we could know what is amiss with each one of the guests assembled here. There is a little man opposite, for instance, who has not spoken once; see, he is writing in a furtive manner in his pocket-book—writing, perhaps, to some one who will be sorry to-morrow to hear what has happened. What on earth brought *him* here? One would have expected that he would have died somewhere in a corner alone. Perhaps he was afraid. There, again, is a man who, to all appearance, is worn out with illness. A fixed pain, perhaps, which is never to be better, and which he can—or will—bear no longer. One would have thought that he would have remained at home. But we all seem afraid to die in solitude, and the Doctor makes everything so very pleasant. Listen; here is a new surprise for us."

Dr. Bertrand was an energetic person, and a man of resource. Not only had he, in consideration of the fog and the rain, caused the fountain to be stopped, and the curtains to be drawn over the entrance to the conservatory, but he had arranged that some musicians should be placed where the flowers used to show, in order that a novel air of luxury might be given to this particular festival. Nor were these, common musicians, whose performance might have infused gloom rather than cheerfulness into the assembly. The Doctor had caused performers of choice ability to be selected, and their music now stole gently on the senses of the guests, and produced an effect that was infinitely agreeable.

"How well this man understands his business," remarked of Clerval to his neighbour. "There is something almost great about him."

There is nothing that varies more in its effect upon us than music; according to the circumstances under which we hear it, it will, to a great extent, prove either stimulating or saddening; still more, of course, does the effect depend upon the music selected. In this case, with the talk already started, with the wine circulating incessantly, with lights flashing in all directions, the effect of the music was exciting in the extreme. And then it had been selected with no common skill. It was not touching

music, such as makes one think; but it was made up of a selection of vigorous gallant tunes that seemed to stir the blood in the veins, and rather agitate the nerves than soothe them.

The music was an experiment which Dr. Bertrand had not tried before, and he watched the effect of it carefully.

De Clerval and his neighbour were silent for a time, partly because they were listening to the music, and also because, for the moment, it was difficult to hear one another. The Doctor's guests were noisy enough now. The wine—the good wine—was doing its work, and loosening the tied-up tongues. What talk it was! Talk of the gaming-table, and the night revel. The horrid infidelity of the time brayed out by throats through which no word of prayer or song of praise had passed since the days of earliest childhood.

De Clerval and his neighbour were pursuing their conversation, when the attention of both was suddenly drawn to the opposite side of the table.

Behind the Doctor's chair there always stood a middle-aged man whose business it was to remain stationary in that place, and to keep a steady eye upon every one at table, in order that the very first sign of anything going wrong with a guest might be instantly observed and acted on. The Doctor's calculations were generally most accurate; still he was human, and occasionally some peculiarity of constitution on the part of one of his patients would defeat him. Or they might partake of certain dishes in continuous succession, some one or two only of which the Doctor had intended to be eaten consecutively. In short, unpleasant things would take place occasionally, and so this special officer was in attendance.

This individual suddenly bent down and drew his master's attention to a gentleman seated at the other end of the table, over whom there had gathered a certain strange rigidity of figure and face. He had dropped his fork, and now sat bolt upright in his chair, staring straight before him with a fixity of gaze and a drop of the lower jaw which Dr. Bertrand understood perfectly well.

"Peste!" said the Doctor. "How cantankerous some exceptional constitutions are! One never knows where to have them. You must not lose a second; call in the others and remove him. He is of an epileptic constitution. Lose not a moment."

The familiar disappeared for an instant, and returned, accompanied by four noiseless men, who followed him swiftly to the end of the table where the wretched guest was seated. He had already begun to shriek aloud, while his features were distorted horribly, and the foam was gathering on his lips.

"Oh, my life!" he screamed. "My lost life! Give it me—I must have it—a loan—it was only a loan! I have frittered it away. I want it back. Only a little of it, then; a very little would be something. Ah, it is this man!" The Doctor was near him now, and the epileptic made a furious attempt to get at him. "This man has got my life, my misspent life—it is going—going from me at his will—my life—my lost——" The miserable creature was overpowered and fainting, and the four noiseless men carried him away. Still, as they bore him through the door, he lifted up his voice again, and cried aloud for his youth—his lost youth—and said he would use it differently if they would give it back to him.

They could hear his screams for some time after that, even in the Doctor's padded and muffled house. The incident was horrible, and produced a state of excitement in the other guests. The noise and uproar which followed this terrible occurrence were hellish; everybody was up in arms at once, and it was upon the Doctor himself that all the indignation fell. What did he mean by it? He was an impostor. They had been brought there under false pretences. They had understood that what was done in that establishment was done decently, done effectually, done with a consideration for the feelings of the guests, done in a gentleman-like manner. Here they were, on the contrary, subjected to a scene which was horrible, disgusting, a thing of the hospitals, a horror!

The Doctor bowed before this storm of invectives. He was deeply, abjectly, miserable at what had occurred: such a thing was rare—rare in the extreme. There were people with constitutions that defied all calculation; people who did not know how to live, nor even how to—— Well, he could only express his profound regret. Would they do him the favour to taste this new wine just brought up? It was Lafitte of a celebrated year, and the Doctor drained off a bumper, by way of setting a good example. It was soon followed by the already half-drunken guests, and the noise and uproar became worse than ever.

"Did you observe what that gentleman partook of?" asked Dr. Bertrand of his familiar. "The gentleman who has just made a scene, I mean?"

"By unlucky chance," was the reply, "he partook in succession of three of your most powerfully *seasoned* dishes. I was thinking—but it is not for me to speak——"

"Yes, yes, it is. What were you thinking?"

"I was thinking, monsieur, whether it was judicious to put three preparations of such great strength next to each other."

"Quite true, quite true," answered the Doctor. "I will make a note of the case."

Meanwhile, De Clerval and his neighbour had fallen again into conversation. There seemed about the stranger something like an interest in his companion. It appeared as if he still thought this dining-room of the Doctor's no place for so young a man.

"If I am too young to be here," said De Clerval, "ought not you, who are of maturer years, to be too wise?"

"No," replied the other; "I have reasoned the thing out, and have thought well and care-

fully of what I am doing. I had one last chance of happiness after many missed or thrown away; the chance has failed me; there is nothing in store; there is nothing possible now that would give me the least satisfaction. The world is of no use to me, and I am of no use in the world."

There was a pause. Perhaps De Clerval felt that under the circumstances there was little room for argument; perhaps he perceived that, to reason against a course which he was himself pursuing, and yet which he felt unaccountably inclined to reason against, was preposterous—at any rate he was silent and the stranger went on:

"It is curious, with regard to certain of one's relatives, how we lose sight of them for a time, a very long time even, and then some circumstance brings one into contact with them, and the intercourse becomes intimate and frequent. It was so with me and my cousin. I had not seen her for years. I had been much away from Paris during those years—in Russia, at Vienna, and elsewhere—engaged in diplomatic service. In all the wild dissipations to be found at the different courts to which I was attached, I engaged with the most dissipated; and when I lately returned to Paris I believed myself to be a totally exhausted man, for whom a veritable emotion was henceforth out of the question. But I was mistaken."

"There is nothing," remarked Alfred, "that men are more frequently mistaken about."

"Well! I was so at any rate," continued the stranger. "After a lapse of many years I met my cousin again, and found in her, qualities so irresistible, so unlike any I had met with in the world, such freshness and truth——"

"There *are* such women on earth," interrupted De Clerval.

"In a word," continued the other, without noticing the interruption, "I came to the conclusion that, could I ally her destiny with mine, there was a new life and a happy one yet in store for me. I believed that I should be able to shake off my old vile garments, get rid of my old bad habits, and—*begin again*. What a vision came up before me of a life in which SHE should lead me and help me, be my guide along a good way better known to her than to me! I determined to make the cast, and that my life should depend on the issue of the throw. It was only yesterday that the cast was made—and the consequence is, that—that I am here."

Alfred was silent; a strange feeling of pity came over him for this man. In spite of his own trouble, there seemed to be a corner in his heart that was sorry yet for his neighbour.

"At that terrible interview," the stranger went on, "I forced the truth from her. Thérèse was not a demonstrative woman. There was a fund of reserve about her which kept her from showing herself to every one. It was a fault, and so was her pride, the besetting sin of those who have never fallen."

From the moment when the name of Thérèse

had been mentioned, the attention of Alfred had been drawn with increased fixity to the narrative to which he was listening. It was with greediness that he now caught at every word which followed.

"I forced the truth from her. I believe she spoke it the less unwillingly because it was her wish to save me from any delusion in the matter, and mercifully to deprive me of hope which could never have any real foundation. I besought her to tell me, in the name of Heaven's truth, was there one in the world more favoured —one who possessed the place in her heart which I had sought to occupy? She hesitated, but I pressed her hard and wrung it from her. Yes, there was one : one who held her heart for ever. I was greedy, I would know all : his name : his condition. And I did. I got to know it all—the history of their love—the name of my rival."

"And what was it ?" asked Alfred, in a voice that seemed to himself like that of another man.

"Alfred de Clerval."

Alfred sprung to his feet, and looked towards the Doctor. "She loves me," he gasped, "and I am *here !*"

The sudden move of De Clerval attracted all attention. "Ah! another !" the guests yelled out. "Another who does not know how to behave himself. Another who is going to scream at us and drive us mad, and die before our very faces !"

"No, no !" cried Alfred. "No, no! not die, but live !' I *must* live. All is changed, and I call upon this Doctor here to save me."

"How do you mean that 'all is changed ?' " whispered the man whose narration had brought all this about. "Changed by what I have said ?"

The noise was so great that De Clerval could not for the moment answer. The self-doomed wretches round the table seemed to feel a horrible jealousy at the idea of an escape. Even the Doctor sought in vain to restore order now.

"Ah, the renegade," cried the guests, "the coward ! He is afraid. He has thought better of it ! Impostor, what did he ever come among us for !"

"Hold ! gentlemen," cried Alfred, in a voice that made the glasses ring ; "I am neither coward nor renegade. I came here to die, because I wished to die. And now I wish to live — not from caprice nor fear, but because the circumstances which made me wish to die, are changed ; because I have learnt the truth but this moment, learnt it in this room, learnt it at this table, learnt it of this gentleman."

"Tell me," said the stranger, now seizing him by the arm, "what had my story to do with all this ? Unless—unless——"

"Monsieur le Vicomte de Noel," replied the other, "I am Alfred de Clerval, and the story you told me was of Thérèse de Farelles. Judge whether I am anxious to live or not."

A frightful convulsion passed over the features of the Vicomte de Noel, and he fell back in his chair.

Meanwhile the uproar continued among Dr. Bertrand's guests.

"We acknowledge nothing," one of the maddened wretches cried, "as a reason for breaking faith with Death. We are all his votaries. We came together in good fellowship to do him honour. Hurrah for Death ! Here is a fellow who would turn infidel to our religion. A renegade, I say again, and what should be the fate of renegades !"

"Follow me without a moment's delay," whispered a voice in Alfred's ear. "You are in the greatest danger."

It was the Doctor's familiar spirit who spoke. Alfred turned to follow him. Then he hesitated, and, hastily leaning down, said these words in De Noel's ear :

"For Heaven's sake don't let your life be sacrificed in this horrible way. Follow me, I entreat you."

"Too late ! It is over," gasped the dying man. He seemed to make an ineffectual effort to say more, and then he spread his arms out on the table, and his head fell heavily upon them.

"You will be too late in another instant," said the Doctor's servant, seizing Alfred hastily by the arm. As De Clerval passed through the side-door which the man opened, such a rush was made towards the place as plainly showed what a narrow escape he had had. The servant, however, locked and bolted the door in time, and those poor half-poisoned and half-drunken wretches were foiled in their purpose.

And now, that escape effected, and the excitement of the previous moment at an end, a strange weakness and giddiness came over De Clerval, and he sunk upon a large sofa to which he had mechanically found his way. The room was a large one, and dimly lighted by a simple lamp, shaded, which stood upon a bureau or escritoire nearly large enough to occupy one end of the room, and covered with papers, bottles, surgical instruments, and other medical lumber. The room was filled with such matters, and it opened into another and a smaller apartment, in which were crucibles, a furnace, many chemical preparations, and a bath which could be heated at the shortest notice.

"The Doctor will. be here himself immediately," said the familiar, approaching De Clerval with a glass, in which was some compound which he had hastily mixed ; "meantime, he bade me give you this."

De Clerval swallowed the mixture, and the attendant left the room. No doubt there was work enough for him elsewhere. Before leaving, however, he told Alfred that he must by all means keep awake.

In compliance with these instructions, and feeling an unwonted drowsiness creeping over him, De Clerval proceeded to walk up and down the room. He was not himself. He would stop, almost without knowing it, in the middle of his promenade, become unconscious for a moment, then would be suddenly and violently roused by finding that his balance was going, and once he did fall. But he sprang up instantly, feeling that his life depended on it. He set himself mental tasks, tasks of memory, or he would try to convince himself that he was in possession of his faculties by reasoning as to where he was, what circumstances had occurred, and the like. "I am in Dr.—Dr.—study," he would say to himself. "I know all about it— waiting to see—waiting, mind, to see—I am waiting—Dr.——" He was falling into a state of insensibility in spite of all his efforts, when Dr. Bertrand, whose approach he had not heard, stood there before him. The sight of the Doctor roused him.

"Doctor, can you save me?"

"First, I must ask *you* a question," replied the Doctor. "It is about one of the dishes at table—now recollect yourself. The 'Curry à l'Anglaise.' Did you partake of it?"

De Clerval was silent for a moment, making a violent effort to collect his bewildered faculties.

At last he remembered something that decided him.

"No, I did not. I remember thinking that an English dish is never good in France, and I let it pass."

"Then," said Dr. Bertrand, "there is good hope. Follow me into this room."

For a long time Alfred de Clerval's life was in the greatest danger. Although he had not partaken of that one particular dish which Dr. Bertrand considered it beyond his power to counteract, he had yet swallowed enough that was poisonous, to make his ultimate recovery exceedingly doubtful. Probably no other man but he who had so nearly caused his death could have saved his life. But Dr. Bertrand knew what was wrong—which is not always the case with doctors—and he also knew how to deal with that wrong. So, after a long and tedious illness and convalescence, Alfred so far recovered as to be able to drop the Doctor's acquaintance, which he was very anxious to do, and to take advantage of the information he had gained from the unfortunate Vicomte de Noel.

Whether Mademoiselle de Farelles was able to pardon the crime her lover had so nearly committed, in consideration of the fact that it was love for her which had led him on to attempt it, I don't know; but my belief is that she did pardon it.

For Dr. Bertrand, his career was a short one. The practices by which he was amassing a large fortune were not long in coming to the knowledge of the police authorities, and in due time it was determined by those who had the power to carry out their conclusions, that it would be for the good of the Doctor's health that the remainder of his life should be passed in the neighbourhood of Cayenne, where, if he chose, he might give dinners to such of the convicts as could be the most easily spared by government.

III.

ANOTHER PAST LODGER RELATES HIS EXPERIENCE AS A POOR RELATION.

The evening was raw and there was snow on the streets, genuine London snow, half-thawed, and trodden, and defiled with mud. I remembered it well, that snow, though it was fifteen years since I had last seen its cheerless face. There it lay, in the same old ruts, and spreading the same old snares on the side-paths. Only a few hours arrived from South America viâ Southampton, I sat in my room at Morley's Hotel, Charing Cross, and looked gloomily out at the fountains, walked up and down the floor discontentedly, and fiercely tried my best to feel glad that I was a wanderer no more, and that I had indeed got home at last.

I poked up my fire, and took a long look backward upon my past life, through the embers. I remembered how my childhood had been embittered by dependence, how my rich and respectable uncle, whose ruling passion was vainglory, had looked on my existence as a nuisance, not so much because he was obliged to open his purse to pay for my clothing and education, as because that, when a man, he thought I could reflect no credit upon his name. I remembered how in those days I had a soul for the beautiful, and a certain almost womanish tenderness of heart, which by dint of much sneering had been successfully extracted from me. I remembered my uncle's unconcealed relief at my determination to go abroad and seek my fortune, the cold good-by of my only cousin, the lonely bitter farewell to England hardly sweetened by the impatient hopes that consumed rather than cheered me—the hopes of name and gold, won by my own exertions, with which I should yet wring from those who despised me, the worthless respect which they denied me now.

Sitting there at the fire, I rang the bell, and the waiter came to me: an old man whose face I remembered. I asked him some questions. Yes, he knew Mr. George Rutland; recollected that many years ago he used to stay at Morley's when he came to London. The old gentleman had always stayed there. But Mr. George was too grand for Morley's now. The family always came to town in the spring, but, at this season, "Rutland Hall, Kent," would be pretty sure to be their address.

Having obtained all the information I desired, I began forthwith to write a letter:

"Dear George,—I dare say you will be as much surprised to see my handwriting as you would be to behold an apparition from the dead. However, you know I was always a ne'er-do-well, and I have not had the grace to die yet. I am ashamed not to be able to announce myself as having returned home with my fortune made; but mishaps will follow the most hard-working and well-meaning. I am still a young man, even though fifteen of the best years of my life may have been lost, and I am willing to devote myself to any worthy occupation. Meantime, I am anxious to see you and yours. A long absence from home and kindred makes one value the grasp of a friendly hand. I shall not wait for your reply to this, but go down to Kent the day after to-morrow, arriving, I believe, about dinner-time. You see I am making myself assured of your welcome for a few weeks, till I have time to look about me.

"I remain, dear George,

"Your old friend and cousin,

"GUY RUTLAND."

I folded this missive and placed it in its envelope. "I shall find out, once for all, what they are made of," I said, complacently, as I wrote the address, "George Rutland, Esq., Rutland Hall, Kent."

It was about seven on a frosty evening when I arrived at the imposing entrance of Rutland Hall. No Cousin George came rushing out to meet me. "Of course not," I thought; "I am unused to their formal manners in this country. He is lying in wait for me on the mat inside." I was admitted by a solemn person as quietly and mechanically as though my restoration to home and kindred were a thing that had happened regularly in his presence every day since his birth. He ushered me into a grand hall, but no mat supported the impatient feet of the dignified master of the house. "Ah!" said I, "even this, perhaps, were scarcely etiquette. No doubt he stands chafing on the drawing-room hearth-rug, and I have little enough time to make myself presentable before dinner." So, resigning myself to circumstances, I meekly followed a guide who volunteered to conduct me to the chamber assigned to my especial use. I had to travel a considerable distance before I reached it. "Dear me!" I remarked to myself when I did reach it, "I had expected to find the rooms in such a house more elegantly appointed than this!"

I made my toilette, and again submitting myself to my guide, was convoyed to the drawing-room door. All the way down stairs I had been conning pleasant speeches with which to greet my kinsfolk. I am not a brilliant person, but I sometimes succeed in pleasing when I try, and on this occasion I had the desire to do my best. The drawing-room door was at the distant end of the hall, and my arrival had been so very quiet, that I conceived my expectant entertainers could hardly be aware of my presence in the house. I thought I should give them a surprise. The door opened and closed upon me, leaving me within the room. I looked around me, and saw—darkness there, and nothing more.

Ah, yes, but there was something more! There was a blazing fire which sent eddying swirls of light through the shadows, and right in the blush of its warmth a little figure was lounging in an easy-chair. The little figure was a girl of apparently about fifteen or sixteen years of age, dressed in a short shabby black frock, who was evidently spoiling her eyes by reading by the firelight. She lay with her head thrown back, a mass of fair curly hair being thus tossed over the velvet cushion on which it rested, while she held her book aloft to catch the light. She was luxuriating in her solitude, and little dreaming of interruption.

She was so absorbed in her book, the door had opened and closed so noiselessly, and the room was so large, that I was obliged to make a sound to engage her attention. She started violently then, and looked up with a nervous fearfulness in her face. She dropped her book, sat upright, and put out her hand, eagerly grasping a thing I had not noticed before, and which leaned against the chair—a crutch. She then got up leaning on it and stood before me. The poor little thing was lame, and had two crutches by her.

I introduced myself, and her fear seemed to subside. She asked me to sit down, with a prim little assumption of at-home-ness, which did not sit upon her with ease. She picked up her book and laid it on her lap; she produced a net from the recesses of her chair, and with a blush gathered up the curls and tucked them into its meshes. Then she sat quiet, but kept her hand upon her crutches, as if she was ready at a moment's notice to limp away across the carpet, and leave me to my own resources.

"Thomson thought there was nobody in the room," she said, as if anxious to account for her own presence there. "I always stay in the nursery, except sometimes when they all go out and I get this room to myself. Then I like to read here."

"Mr. Rutland is not at home?" I said.

"No, they are all out dining."

"Indeed! Your papa, perhaps, did not get my letter?"

She blushed crimson.

"I am not a Miss Rutland," she said. "My name is Teecie Ray. I am an orphan. My father was a friend of Mr. Rutland, and he takes care of me for charity."

The last word was pronounced with a certain controlled quiver of the lip. But she went on. "I don't know about the letter, but I heard a gentleman was expected. I did not think it could be to-night, though, as they all went out."

"A reasonable conclusion to come to," I thought, and thereupon began musing on the eagerness of welcome displayed by my affectionate Cousin George. If I were the gentleman expected, they must have received my letter, and in it were fully set forth the day and hour of my proposed arrival. "Ah! George, my dear fellow," I said, "you are not a whit changed!"

Arriving at this conclusion, I raised my glance, and met, full, the observant gaze of a pair of large shrewd grey eyes. My little hostess for the time being was regarding me with such a curiously legible expression on her face, that I could not but read it and be amused. It said plainly: "I know more about you than you think, and I pity you. You come here with expectations which will not be fulfilled. There is much mortification in store for you. I wonder you came here at all. If I were once well outside these gates, I should never limp inside them again. If I knew a road out into the world you come from, I would set out bravely on my crutches. No, not even for the sake of a stolen hour like this, in a velvet chair, would I remain here."

How any one glance could say all this, was a riddle; but it did say all this. The language of the face was as simple to me as though every word had been translated into my ear. Perhaps a certain internal light, kindled long ago, before this little orphan was born, or George Rutland had become owner of Rutland Hall, assisted me in deciphering so much information so readily. However that may be, certain things before surmised became assured facts in my mind, and a quaint bond of sympathy became at once established between me and my companion.

"Miss Ray," I said, "what do you think of a man who, having been abroad for fifteen years, has the impudence to come home without a shilling in his pocket? Ought he not to be stoned alive?"

"I thought how it was," said she, shaking her head, and looking up with another of her shrewd glances. "I knew it, when they put you into such a bad bedroom. They are keeping all the good rooms for the people who are coming next week. The house will be full for Christmas. It won't do," she added, meditatively.

"What won't do?" I said.

"Your not having a shilling in your pocket. They'll sneer at you for it, and the servants will find it out. I have a guinea that old Lady Thornton gave me on my birthday, and if you would take the loan of it I should be very glad. I don't want it at all, and you could pay me back when you are better off."

She said this with such business-like gravity, that I felt obliged to control my inclination to laugh. She had evidently taken me under her protection. Her keen little wits foresaw snares and difficulties besetting my steps during my stay at Rutland Hall, to which my newer eyes, she imagined, must be ignorantly blind. I looked at her with amusement, as she sat there seriously considering my financial interests. I had a fancy to humour this quaint confidential relation that had sprung up so spontaneously between us. I said gravely:

"I am very much obliged to you for your offer, and will gladly take advantage of it. Do you happen to have the guinea at hand?"

She seized her crutches, and limped quickly out of the room. Presently she returned with a little bon-bon box, which she placed in my hand. Opening it, I found one guinea, wrapped up carefully in silver paper.

"I wish it had been more!" she said, wistfully, as I coolly transferred it to my pocket, box and all. "But I so seldom get money!"

At this moment, the solemn person who had escorted me hither and thither before, announced that my dinner was served.

On my return to the drawing-room, I found, to my intense disappointment, that my beneficent bird had flown. Teecie Ray had limped off to the nursery.

Next morning, at breakfast, I was introduced to the family. I found them, on the whole, pretty much what I had expected. My Cousin George had developed into a pompous portly paterfamilias; and, in spite of his cool professions of pleasure, was evidently very sorry to see me. The Mamma Rutland just countenanced me, in a manner the most frigidly polite. The grown-up young ladies treated me with the most well-bred negligence. Unless I had been very obtuse indeed, I could scarcely have failed to perceive the place appointed for me in Rutland Hall. I was expected to sit below the salt. I was that dreadful thing—a person of no importance. George amused himself with me for a few days, displaying to me his various fine possessions, and then, on the arrival of grander guests, left me to my own resources. The Misses Rutland endured my escort on their riding expeditions only till more eligible cavaliers appeared. As for the lady of the house, her annoyance at having me quartered indefinitely on her premises, was hardly concealed. The truth was, they were new people in the circle in which they moved, and it did not suit them to have a poor relation coming suddenly among them, calling them "cousin," and making himself at home in the house. For me, I was not blind, though none of these things did it suit me to see. I made myself as comfortable as was possible under the circumstances, took every sneer and snub in excellent part, and was as amiable and satisfied on all occasions as though I believed myself to be the most cherished inmate of the household. That this meanness of mine should provoke their contempt, I had hardly a right to complain of. Nor did I. I accepted this like the rest of their hospitality, and smiled contentedly as the days went on. The gloom which had oppressed me on my first arrival in England had all betaken itself away. How could I feel otherwise than supremely happy at finding myself thus surrounded by my kind relations, thus generously entertained under their hospitable roof?

As I found that the guests at Rutland Hall enjoyed a certain freedom in their choice of amusements, and the disposal of their time, I speedily availed myself of this privilege. I selected my own associates, and I entertained myself as pleased me best. Not finding myself always welcomed in the drawing-room, I contrived, by a series of the most dexterous artifices, to gain the free entrée of the nursery. In this nursery were growing up, some five or six younger branches of the Rutland family. After a certain hour in the day none of the elders ever thought of invading its remote precincts. Five o'clock in the evening was the children's tea-hour, and the pleasantest, I thought, in the twenty-four. Nurse was a staid woman, who knew how to appreciate a little present now and again, and to keep her own counsel on the subject. The children were not pleasant children; they were unruly mischievous little wretches. They conceived a sort of affection for me, because I sometimes brought to the nursery, sundry purchases made during solitary rides; picture-books, tops, dolls, or sweetmeats, procured by means of Teecie Ray's guinea. I suggested as much to Teecie one evening as she sat by, watching the distribution, and she nodded her head in sage satisfaction. She thought that I economised my substance very well. It covered a great many small extravagances, that guinea did.

Whatever might be my position at Rutland Hall, Teecie Ray's was simply intolerable. A spirit less brave must have been cowed and broken by it: a nature less delicate must have been blunted and made coarser. The servants openly neglected her, the children used her as they pleased; wreaked their humours on her, sparing neither blow nor taunt in their passions, and demanding from her at all times whatever service it suited their capricious fancy to need. Nurse, the only one who ever showed a grain of consideration for the orphan, would sometimes shield her from their impish attacks, when she could do so with safety to herself; but she was not permitted to deal with those darlings in the only fashion which would have been at all likely to bring them to reason. As for the elders of the house, Teecie Ray's momentary presence, or the mere mention of her name, was sufficient to ruffle their peace of mind. "What is to be done with that girl?" I heard Mrs. Rutland remark to one of her daughters. "If she were not lame, one might set her to earn her bread in some way; but, as it is——" A shrug of the shoulders, and a certain vinegar-like expression of countenance, which this lady knew how to assume, sufficiently developed the idea thus imperfectly expressed.

And how did Teecie Ray meet all this? She did not complain nor rebel, she did not sulk nor fret. Under that well-worn black frock of hers, she carried a little breastplate of sober determined endurance. When sorely tried, there was never any cowardly submission to be seen in her grave little face, neither was there ever in her manner or words either reproach or remonstrance. She simply endured. Her large patient eyes and mute wise mouth seemed to say, "Whatever I suffer, whatever I long to dare, gratitude shackles my limbs, and seals my lips. I am saved from many things; therefore I am dumb."

The second time I met my little benefactress, was a day or two after our first interview in the drawing-room. I came upon her, one afternoon by chance, limping down a hedge lane which lay to the back of the house, away beyond the gardens, and the kitchen gardens, and the pleasure-grounds. This lane, I found, led to a large meadow, and beyond the meadow there was a wooded hill, and far down at the distance of the hill there was a river. This was Teecie Ray's favourite ramble, and her one avenue of escape from the torments of the nursery. I immediately began pouring forth a legion of perplexing troubles and difficulties, to all of which she listened with perfect credulity, expressing her sympathy as I went along by an expressive nod of the head, or a shrewd swift glance. Then she gave me her wise little counsel when all was told, and went home, I believe, pondering on my case.

As the days passed, and my relations became more and more involved in their winter gaieties, I found myself more and more thrown upon my own resources for amusement. Occasionally I was included in an invitation, and accepted it; but in general I preferred indulging my fancy for keeping aloof from those who were little charmed with my company. A system of the most unblushing bribery had won for me a warm welcome from the savage tribes in the nursery. Many and many an evening found me walking down that hedged lane in the frosty dusk, with Teecie Ray limping by my side, and talking her grave simple little talk. I had always some fresh puzzle to propose to her, and she was always ready to knit her smooth brows over its solution. Once she stopped short, and struck her little crutches on the snow.

"You ought to go away from here and work," she cried. "O, if I could!"

A certain Sir Harry arrived at Rutland Hall; I will not trouble myself to think of his second name; it is not worth remembering. He was a wealthy bachelor of high family, and his movements were watched with interest by the lady of the house. This Sir Harry had a fancy for smoking his cigar in the hedged lane, and on more than one occasion he encountered my little benefactress limping on her solitary way, and stared at the pretty fresh face under her old black hat, till it blushed with uncomfortable brilliance. Teecie changed her track like a hunted hare, but Sir Harry scented her out, and annoyed her with his fulsome compliments. The matter reached Mrs. Rutland's ears, and she vented her chagrin on the defenceless little girl. I know not what sorry accusations and reproaches she bestowed upon her during a long private lecture; but, that evening when, at the children's tea-hour, I entered the nursery door with a new ball in my hand for Jack (the youngest and least objectionable of the band), I saw Teecie Ray's face grievously clouded for the first time. It was flushed and swollen with passionate crying. I do not intend to commit to paper certain remarks which I made sotto voce on beholding this disfigurement.

"Come, come, Teecie," I said, while nurse was busy quelling a disturbance which had arisen because "Cousin Guy" had not brought something to every one else as well as Jack; "where is all your philosophy, little mother? You need never preach to me again, if you set me such a bad example."

Teecie said never a word, but stared on into the fire. This wound had cut deep. Sir Harry, and Mrs. Rutland, of Rutland Hall, at that moment I should have dearly loved to knock your two good-for-nothing heads together!

"Teecie," I said, "you have one friend, at any rate, even if he be not a very grand one."

She gave one of her quaint expressive little nods. Translated, it meant: "I understand all that, but I cannot talk just now." By-and-by, however, she brightened up, and went to the table to claim her share of tea and thick bread-and-butter, and I began to mend a bow belonging to Tom. Tom was one of the leaders of the unruly tribes, a regular savage chieftain.

Ere two days more had passed I felt strongly inclined to exercise the horsewhip on this young gentleman's shoulders. Tom, one fine morning, was seized with an impish inspiration to play a trick upon Teecie. Stealing her crutches, he walked about the nursery mimicking her poor little limp, and then marching off with them, heedless of her entreaties to have them restored, carried them in triumph out of doors, and smashed them in pieces with a hatchet. Teecie sat helpless in the din and riot of that ill-conditioned nursery. Bright bracing days came and found her a prisoner, looking with longing eyes through the window-panes, out over the beautiful country lanes. Tom saw her patience with the most audacious indifference. But why talk about Tom? I could not help believing, nor do I ever intend to help believing, that older heads than Tom's plotted the cruel caging of that bonnie bird.

The bird drooped on its perch; but who cared? Nurse vowed it was a shame, and showed more kindness than usual to the prisoner, but I will not venture to decide how much of this tenderness was owing to the odd crown-pieces which found their way from my hand to hers—all out of the guinea, of course? O yes, all out of the guinea. And there was another friend who sometimes expressed an interest in Teecie Ray's existence. This was that Lady Thornton, whose bounty had indirectly furnished me with pocket-money during my stay at Rutland Hall. The favour of this old lady I had done my best to win. She was a nice comfortable old lady, and I liked her. It happened that she called one day during Teecie Ray's imprisonment, to invite the Rutlands and their visitors, great and small, young and old, to a party to be given at her house, a few miles distant. I chanced to be alone in the drawing-room when she arrived, and I seized the opportunity to tell her the story of Teecie's crutches.

"A bad boy!" she said. "A bad, malicious boy! She must get new crutches before my party."

"Of course she must," I said, very heartily.

The old lady threw back her head, raising her fat chin in a peculiar sort of way, and looking at me direct through her spectacles.

"Indeed!" she said. "Pray, young man, what particular interest do you take in Teecie Ray?"

I smiled. "Oh, Teecie and I are excellent friends," I said.

"Teecie and you!" she repeated. "Pray, are you aware that Miss Ray is eighteen years of age?"

"Is she indeed? I know nothing about the ages of little girls."

"But Teecie is not a little girl, Mr. Guy Rutland. Teecie Ray is a woman, I tell you!"

Teecie Ray a woman! I could not help laughing. What? My little benefactress, my little mother! I am afraid I scandalised Lady Thornton on that occasion by my utter scorn of her proposition. Christina Rutland swept into the room at this crisis, and relieved me in my difficulty. But often afterwards during that day, I laughed when I thought of Lady Thornton's piece of information. Teecie Ray a woman? Preposterous!

One morning, when it wanted but a week of the party, a curious event occurred. The heads of the house met in consultation on the matter, in the library, before breakfast. An extraordinary Thing had arrived from London at Rutland Hall. The Thing was a large wooden case, directed to Teecie Ray. On being eagerly opened, it was found to contain a pair of crutches.

And such a pair of crutches! Light and symmetrical, and fanciful, works of art in their way. Tortoiseshell stems with silver mountings of exquisite workmanship, capped with dainty little cushions of embroidered velvet. Thunder-stricken were the elders of the house. "Who could have done this thing?" was on every lip. Who, indeed? Who outside of Rutland Hall had ever heard of Teecie Ray? These crutches were costly affairs. I knew the conclusion they came to, one and all. They pitched on Sir Harry as the culprit. It was a thorn in their side, and I rubbed my hands in glee.

Having considered the question in their dismay, they decided that Teecie should be kept in ignorance of her mysterious present. It was not fit for her to use, it would fill her mind with absurd ideas. And so, in spite of the arrival of her beautiful new crutches, poor Teecie still sat helpless in the nursery. The wooden case and its contents were hidden away, and no word was spoken of their existence.

I waited a few days to see if the elders would relent, but to no purpose. The bird still pined on its perch. No kindly hand seemed likely to open the cage door and let it fly. There sat Teecie, day after day, in her nursery chair, hemming aprons for nurse, or darning the children's stockings, looking longingly out of the window, and growing pale for want of fresh air. Still never rebelling, never complaining. Meantime the stir of Christmas preparation was agitating all the household, and the children were full of rapture at the prospect of Lady Thornton's Christmas party. There was great excitement in the nursery about pretty new dresses, wonderful fussing about ribbons, and muslins, and fripperies. Teecie alone sat silent in her shabby frock. By-and-by, her hands were full, bowing up sashes, sewing on tuckers, stitching rosettes on shoes. She was a nimble little workwoman, and they kept her busy. Seeing how well a lapful of bright ribbons became her, I thought it a pity she should not have a gay dress as well as the rest.

Nobody said, "Teecie, what will you wear?" nor even, "Teecie, are not you invited too?" No one seemed to expect for a moment that Teecie could wish to be merry with the rest. How could she go, she who was lame and had no crutches?

It happened that I had an errand to the nearest town. It was rather late when, on my return, I called at the best millinery establishment in the place, and asked for a parcel.

Yes, the parcel was ready. A large flat box. "Would the gentleman like to see the lady's pretty dress?" The box was opened, and a cloud of some airy fabric shaken out under my eyes. I cannot, of course, describe it, but it was something white, very pure and transparent, with something else of pink just blushing through it. It was very tasteful, I pronounced, trying to look wise. There was only one fault: "Did it not seem rather long for a little girl?" I asked, remembering the figure it was to adorn, with its short skirt just coming to the top of the boots, so well worn and mended.

"Oh, sir," said the milliner, with dignity, "you said the young lady was eighteen years of age, and of course we have given her a flowing skirt!"

It was late in the evening when I reached home. Two merry carriage-fulls were just departing from the door as I drove up. A few minutes afterwards, I was in the nursery with the milliner's parcel in my hands. There sat dear little Cinderella, resting one flushed cheek on her hand, and contemplating the litter of scraps of ribbon, fragments of lace, scissors, flowers, and reels of cotton, which lay scattered around her. She had had a toilsome tiresome day, and now they had got all they wanted of her, and had left her to her solitude.

A flash of pleasure sprang to her face when she saw me. "Oh! I thought you had gone with the rest," she said.

"No," said I, "I have not gone yet, but I am going presently. I came for you."

"For me!" she echoed in dismay. "You know I could not go. I have no dress, even if I could walk."

"A friend has sent you a dress," I said, "and I will undertake to provide the crutches. Nurse, will you please to take this box, and get Miss Teecie ready as quickly as possible. The carriage is waiting for us at the door."

Teecie flushed very red at first, and I thought she was going to burst out crying, and then she turned pale, and looked frightened. Nurse, to whom I had slipped a munificent Christmas-box, immediately fell into raptures over the pretty dress.

"Come, Teecie," I said, "make haste!" And, trembling between dread and delight, Teecie suffered herself to be carried off to her toilette.

By the time I returned from an exploring expedition, with the wonderful silver-and-tortoise-shell crutches under my arm, Teecie was ready.

Teecie was ready. Those three simple little words mean so much that I feel I must stop and

try to translate them into all they are bound to convey. They do not mean that Teecie, the child whom I was wont to call my little benefactress, my little mother, had got on a nice new frock, and was equipped for a juvenile party like other children. But they mean that there, when I came back, stood a beautiful girl by the nursery fire, in a fair sweeping blush-coloured robe. When she turned her head, I saw that the sweet face framed in its childlike curls was the same, but still the old Teecie Ray was gone, and here was (*peccavi* Lady Thornton!) a lovely woman.

We were all three ludicrously amazed at the sudden metamorphose that had taken place. Teecie was too simple not to show that she felt the change in herself, felt it keenly, with a strange delight and a strange shyness. Nurse had so long been accustomed to use her as a child that she stood bewildered. As for me, I was first frightened at what I had done, then enchanted, then foolishly awkward, and almost as shy as Teecie herself.

When I presented the crutches, nurse looked at me as though I must be some prince in disguise, out of the Arabian Nights. It was with a curious feeling that I saw Teecie try them, not limping now, rather gliding over the nursery floor, with the little velvet cushions hidden away amidst clouds of lace and muslin under her round white shoulders, and the airy masses of the fresh tinted gown just crushed back a little by the gleaming silver staves. I don't know why it was that I thought at that moment, with a certain rapture, of a guinea in a little bon-bon box, that lay below in the one shabby portmanteau which I had thought proper to bring with me to Rutland Hall!

Our equipage awaited us. It was too late now to withdraw from what I had undertaken. Teecie and I were soon dashing over the snowy roads to Lady Thornton's. I will not attempt to describe the remainder of that memorable evening, or the sensation caused by our arrival; the wonder and mortification of my kind relations; or the mingled pleasure and displeasure of the hostess, who, while delighted to see her little favourite, took occasion to whisper angrily in my ear, "And pray, sir, how is all this to end?"

The scene was all new and delightful to Teecie, but her dread of Mrs. Rutland's portentous frown would not let her enjoy it. We both felt that a storm would burst over our heads that night, and we were not wrong. None of the family from Rutland Hall took the least notice of us. When the time came for going home, they went off in their two carriages, and Teecie and I drove home as we had come. When we arrived, we found Cousin George and his wife waiting for us in the library, armed to the teeth. I saw it was to be war and no quarter. Mrs. Rutland took Teecie into her clutches, and carried her off, and I was left with George. I need not repeat all that passed between us.

"Sir," he said, "we have suffered your insolent intrusion long enough. You leave this house to-morrow morning."

"Cousin George," I said, "don't put yourself in a passion. I will go to-morrow morning, but upon one condition—that Teecie Ray may come with me, if she will."

He looked at me perfectly aghast. "Do you know," he said, "that she is a penniless friendless orphan, whom I have sheltered through charity?"

"I want to make her my wife," I said, sternly, "if, indeed, I be so fortunate as to have won her affections."

"And after that," he said, with a sneer "how do you propose to live? Upon air, or your friends?"

"Not upon you, George Rutland," I said, looking him steadily in the eyes. "Mark me. I have tried you out. I have sifted you, all in this house, like a handful of wheat. I found you all chaff, but the one golden grain which lies on my palm. I will keep it and treasure it, if I may. God grant I may!"

"Very fine," said George, "very fine. Remember, however, that from this moment I wash my hands of you both: you, Guy Rutland, and her, Teecie Ray."

"Amen!" I said, and bade him good night, and turned on my heel and left him.

Early next morning I knocked at the nursery door, and begged of nurse to awake Miss Teecie, and ask her to speak with me in the garden. I then went out to wait for her. It was Christmas morning, the day of peace and good will. What I felt was scarcely peace, as I looked over the calm landscape. And yet I bore no ill will to any man or woman.

Teecie came to me by-and-by; just the same old Teecie, limping over the frosty path in her short shabby frock, and looking half ashamed of her grand new crutches. I felt relieved when I saw her so. I was shy of the dainty lady whom I had called into existence the night before. And yet when I looked more closely, I knew that this was not quite the old Teecie, and that the very same Teecie of a day ago never, never, could come back. Something was altered. Whether the change was in her or me, or in both of us, I did not inquire. The change was not an unpleasant one.

We strolled out of the garden, and into the lane, and we talked earnestly all the way. On our way back I said:

"And you're not afraid of starving with me, Teecie? You'll take the risk?"

One of her old nods was Teecie's answer.

"Go and fetch your hat, then," said I, "and we won't even wait for breakfast. Don't bring anything else with you, not a shred. I have still some halfpence left—out of the guinea, you know—and we'll get all we want."

Teecie fetched her hat and returned, and we set off together. An hour afterwards we were man and wife. We said our prayers side by side in the church, and then we walked back to Rutland Hall, to say good-by to our kinsfolk. I believe they all thought me mad, and her a little fool;—at least until Cousin George received the cheque, which I sent him next day; a cheque to cover the expenses

incurred by him through his charity to Teecie Ray. Then they began to wonder, and to waver. I took my wife abroad, and showed her the world. Time and care cured her of her lameness. It was not surprising that on her return to England her kinsfolk should scarcely recognise her—Teecie Rutland, née Ray—walking without crutches, and the wife of a millionnaire! Half a bride-cake conciliated Lady Thornton, and the wonderful guinea is still in my possession. I call it Teecie's dower. The crutches, the donor of which I beg to assure you, major, was *not* Sir Harry, are also preserved as family curiosities.

IV.

ANOTHER PAST LODGER RELATES
WHAT LOT HE DREW AT GLUMPER HOUSE.

If the dietary at Doctor Glumper's could not be pronounced purely Spartan in its principles, it was simply that the Spartan stomach—well disciplined as we know it to have been—would have revolted at such treatment. Salamis demanded other stamina than could be supplied by the washings of a beef-bone. Xerxes was not deified under the immediate inspiration of rice-dumpling.

Doctor Glumper's was not much worse, in its commissariat, my dear Major Jackman, than hundreds of other establishments, at which—in those days—the sons of gentlemen studied and starved. There was enough to live upon, provided we could have fairly eaten what there *was*. Therein lay the difficulty. Our meals, bad enough at the beginning of the week, grew gradually worse towards the end: insomuch that we arrived at the Sabbath, much in the condition of a band of young seafarers, who had been cast away, and were only saved from utter starvation by the opportune arrival of a ship freighted with roast-beef and Yorkshire pudding.

True, there was a life-boat. It's name, in our case, was "Hannah's Basket." Hannah was the laundress, and, on Saturday afternoon, after delivering the linen, regularly made her appearance in the playground, displaying the bottom of her buck-basket paved with delicacies, carefully selected on the principle of combining the three grand qualities of sweetness, stickiness, and economy.

Elegance and refinement were little thought of, in those days. The boy who brought a silver fork, would have been simply regarded as possessed of a jocular turn. As for the spoon and six towels, which, according to the printed terms of Glumper House, seemed absolutely essential to a sound classical education—the spoon found its way into a species of armoury of Mrs. Glumper's, formed of the spoils of the young Philistines, her pupils, prohibited toys, confiscated literature, and so forth; while the towels, absorbed in the general republic of that article, passed into indiscriminate use. Well, we had nothing to say against steel forks. The meat, peradventure, might have proved impervious to any less undaunted metal.

Our Monday's dinner was boiled leg of mutton. One helping. More was not refused; but the ill-concealed impatience with which the application was received, established the custom of contenting ourselves with what was first supplied. The due reward of this pusillanimity appeared on the following day, in the form of half-consumed joints—cold, ghastly, seamed with red murderous streaks, and accompanied by certain masses of ill-washed cabbage, interesting as an entomological study; but, as a viand, repulsive by reason of the caterpillars, whose sodden dull-green corpses I have seen lying in ranks beside the plates of fastidious feeders.

Three days a week, we had rice-pudding—a confection which, by an unfortunate conjuncture of circumstances, I never could from infancy endure; but the great trial of our lives, and stomachs, was reserved for Saturday, when we sat down to what was satirically styled a "beef-steak-pie."

Mean and debased must be the spirit of that bullock who would confess to any share in such a production! Into the composition of that dish beef entered as largely as the flesh of the unicorn into peas-porridge. The very wildness of the rumours that were afloat respecting its actual origin proved how dark, difficult, and mysterious was the inquiry. School tradition pointed to the most grotesque and inharmonious elements, as actually detected in the pie. Substances, in texture, flavour, and appearance, the reverse of bovine, had been over and over again deposed to by the dismayed recipients, who proved their good faith by preferring famine itself to "beef-steak"-pie. The utter impossibility of identifying the ingredients as having pertained to any animal recognised by British cooks, was the terrific feature of the case.

Whatever was the prevailing element of the pie, it was supplemented with minor matters, about which, though they do not appear in any accepted recipe for the dish in question, there could be no dispute.

Sholto Shillito, for instance, who had the appetite of an ogre, boldly swallowed the portion assigned him, but quietly and sternly removed to the side of his plate three fingers and a ligament of the thumb of an ancient dog-skin glove.

Billy Duntze discovered and secreted something that was for several halves preserved in the school as the leg of a flamingo. At all events, it was introduced, so labelled, to every new arrival, on the very first evening of his sojourn among us.

George van Kempen found a pair of snuffers.

Charley Brooksbank remarked a singular protuberance in his portion of pie, and, carefully excavating the same, as if it were a Phœnician relic, brought to light something that looked like the head of a doll that had been afflicted with hydrocephalus. On being cut into, it was green. For the first few weeks of each half—that is, while our pocket-money held out—we got on

pretty well. Our pocket-money exhausted, starvation stared us in the face.

The present generation may wonder why we did not try the effect of respectful remonstrance. The times, as I have said, were different then, and besides, the present generation didn't personally know Mrs. Glumper. A fearful woman was Mrs. Glumper. I don't mean that she raved, struck, or demeaned herself in any way not ordinarily witnessed in polite society; but I do mean that she had a cool quiet scorn, a consciousness of a putting-down power, as though an elephant, just tickling the ground with a foot as big as a writing-table, were to show how easily and effectually he might, if he pleased, turn that table upon you.

In addition to this overbearing contempt, Mrs. Glumper had a thousand ways of making us uncomfortable, without resorting to overt tyranny; insomuch that to be "out of favour" with that excellent lady was regarded as the climax of school misery.

Not a word have I to say against the doctor. Even then I felt him to be a good man. In remembering his character, I believe him to have been one of the best that ever breathed. With the understanding of a sage, he was as simple as a child; so simple, that it was matter of genuine astonishment that he retained the coat upon his back; so simple, that the circumstance of his having espoused Mrs. G. became almost intelligible. For this guileless act, rumour even supplied the motive. Mrs. Glumper, then Miss Kittiewinkle, was herself the mistress of an extremely preparatory school, and it was in the cowed and miserable victims of her Muscovite rule that the kind doctor read an invitation of the most pressing kind, to take the mistress under his. The consequence of this union of interests was, that the establishment, losing its infantine character, flourished up into a school of seventy boys; only the very smallest of whom were submitted to Mrs. Glumper's immediate dominion.

Affairs were in this unsatisfactory position towards the middle of a certain half. It was precisely the period at which the greatest impecuniosity usually prevailed. Money was tighter than any one could recollect. Hannah's breadstuffs were in a condition of blockade. Could "shirtings" have been exchanged for eatings, Hannah might have done a brisk business in turn-downs, but the old lady was too wary for such traffic.

We held a consultation. The doctor's cow, which sometimes grazed in the playing-field, was incidentally present, and by her sleek contented aspect, excited universal disgust.

"Crib her oilcake!" squeaked a voice from the outer senatorial circle.

"It is well for the honourable felon on the back benches," remarked our president, Jack Rogers, who delighted to give to our consultations the aspect of a grave debate, "that his skull is beyond punching-distance. If the oilcake, lavished on yonder pampered animal, had been vested in trustees, to the sole and separate use, notwithstanding coverture, of *Mrs.* Glumper—I—well, I will go so far as to say this council might have taken into consideration what has fallen from the distinguished thief. But it's Glumper's, and the proposal of the estimable criminal will be received with the contempt it deserves."

A murmur of approval greeted this speech, after which sundry suggestions were offered.

Burned pens (Gus Halfacre remarked) were edible. He *might* say, toothsome.

"My left boot is at the service of the commonwealth," said Frank Lightfoot. "The right, having been recently repaired and thickened, and being devoid of a large nail in the sole (of which I invite the state to take heed), I reserve to myself for the last extremity."

"Thus extremes *will* meet," observed the president. "But this is no season for jesting. Has anybody anything to propose?"

"We have always Murrell Robinson," said Sholto Shillito, gloomily, and with an aspect so wolfish, that the young gentleman alluded to—a plump rosy child of eight, who had not yet had time to dwindle—set up a howl of terror.

"It might—humph—yes, it might be politic," said the chairman, thoughtfully. "'Twould touch her home. If Jezebel Glumper lost a couple, say, of pupils, under the peculiar circumstances glanced at by the honourable senator in the inky corduroys, she might have some—shall I say bowels?—for those of the remainder. But the observation of my honourable friend has suggested to my mind a course of action which, though in some respects similar, and promising the like results, is not open to the same objections. Some fellow must *bolt*, placing on record his reasons for that step."

Jack's proposal, unexpected as it was, met with considerable favour, the only difficulty being to decide who the fugitive should be. Bolting from school by no means implied return to the paternal mansion. Everybody looked inquiringly at his neighbour. No one volunteered.

The chairman surveyed us with mournful severity.

"There was once," he faltered, "an individual, known to you all (except the fifth class)—wept over by some—who, on learning that he might greatly benefit certain public property by jumping into a hole, asked no questions, popped in, and did it. Has our school no Curtius? Must seventy stomachs languish unsatisfied for want of a single heart? Shillito, you greedy young beggar, *you* will go."

Mr. Shillito emphatically invoked benediction on himself, in the event of his doing anything of the kind.

"Percy Pobjoy," said the president, "you are one at odds with fortune. You are penniless—worse, for your week's pay, old chap, is impounded for a month. You have sailed into the extreme north of Mrs. Glumper's favour, and are likely to make it your persistent abode. You detest rice,

You have scruples concerning caterpillars. Percival, my friend, three ladies of eminence, whose names and office are fully recorded in your classical dictionary, unanimously select *you* as the party to perform this public service."

Mr. Pobjoy regretted to run counter to the anticipations of *any* lady, but, possessing, as he did, a grandmother who would, he conceived, prove more than a match for the three Destinies—and he would throw the Furies in—he must deny himself the gratification proposed.

"Then," resumed the president, cheerfully, with the air of having at last secured his man, "I at once address myself to the distinguished senator on the inverted flower-pot. He who licked that bully, the miller's boy, in twelve minutes and a half, will be again our champion. Joles will go."

Mr. Joles somewhat sullenly failed to perceive the analogy between pitching into a cheeky clown, and running away from school. Could the honourable president detect the smallest indication of verdure in his (Mr. J.'s) sinister organ of vision? Such a contingency was, nevertheless, essential to his (Mr. J.'s) adopting the course required of him.

Other honourable senators having, when appealed to, returned answers of a no less discouraging character, there seemed to be but one course remaining—that of drawing lots. A resolution to do this was carried, after some discussion: it being agreed that he on whom the lot might fall should decamp on the morrow, and, having found some secure hiding-place, write to one of his schoolmates, or (perhaps preferably) to his own friends, declaring that the step he had taken was prompted by a reluctance to perish of starvation.

The proposed time was subsequently extended to one week, in order that he who drew the fatal lot might have time to try the effect of a touching appeal to his parents or friends, fairly setting forth the treatment we were experiencing. If this answered, well and good. If not, the honourable gentleman (said our chief) "will cut his lucky this day se'nnight."

Lots were then solemnly drawn, in the primitive Homeric fashion, every boy's name—those of the fifth class excepted—being inscribed in a slip of paper, and flung into a hat. There was a strong feeling in favour of exempting Jack Rogers, our president—the Nestor of the school—who, being near seventeen, and about to leave, would, no doubt, have preferred fighting through the remainder of his term, famish as he might. But the good fellow flounced at the idea, as though it had been an insult, and himself cast in his name.

Carefully following our classic model, the hat was then violently shaken. The lot that, in obedience to a fillip from the Fates, first leaped out and touched the earth, was to decide the question. *Two* flew out, but one of these rested on the shaker's sleeve. There was a decided disinclination to take up the other. It seemed as if nobody had, until this supreme crisis, fully realised the consequences that might ensue from thus abandoning at once both school and home.

My heart, I confess, stood still for a moment, as Jack Rogers stood forward and picked up the paper. Then I felt the blood mount to my cheeks, as our leader slowly read, "Charles Stuart Trelawny."

"Always in luck, Charley!" he continued, laughing; but I think Jack only intended to keep up my spirits. "Write directly, my boy," he added, in a graver tone, "and, take my advice, write bang up to the governor. Treat it as a matter of business. Mamma is safe to put in *her* word."

I wrote at once:

"My dear Papa,—I hope you are quite well. I ain't. You know I'm not greedy, and not so foolish as to expect at school such jolly things as at home. So you must not be angry when I say what I'm *obliged* to say, that we can't eat what Mrs. Glumper says is dinner; and as there's nothing else but slop and a bit of bread, everybody's starving.

"I remain, your dutiful Son,
"C. S. TRELAWNY.

"P.S. If you don't like to speak to Mrs. Glumper, would you mind asking mamma and Agnes, with my love, to send me a big loaf of bread (with Crust, and, if possible, browned) that might last a week?

"Lieut.-Gen. Trelawny, C.B., K.H.,
Peurhyn Court."

I thought this despatch sufficiently business-like, and waited with some anxiety for the result. If papa only knew what depended on his decision! He *ought* to put faith in me, for I had never been untruthful, and had done myself no more than justice in reminding him that I was no glutton.

It was, I believe, on the fourth day of suspense that a large parcel was brought into the playground, a crowd of curious and expectant youths escorting it, and witnessing its delivery. Small blame to them!

There resided within the limits of that parcel —for, though mighty, it *had* its limits—first, a beefsteak-pie, not only composed of real beef, but enriched with eggs and minor excellences, all trembling in a jellied gravy of surpassing savour. There was, secondly, a chosen company of mince-pies, clinging together from sheer richness, in such wise that a very stoic, if hungry, might be reluctant to "sever such sweet friends," and devour them two at a time.

There was revealed, in the third place, a large apple turnover: so called, I should surmise, because a boy might turn it over and over, and back again, and, after all, find himself unable to determine which looked the more enticing—the sugary, or the buttery side. And, finally, there was a cake which I can scarcely repent having characterised, at the moment, as "tremendous!"

There was no letter, but the augury seemed good. Such ambassadors as pies and turnovers speak with tongues of their own. It was *not* intended that we should perish. We should see

the effect of my manly and business-like appeal, perhaps that very day, in an improved bill of fare, and a diminution of caterpillars. As to husbanding our new supplies, such an idea never occurred to any one. Alas, that we could not *all* partake! Lots had to be once more drawn, and a lucky party of eighteen, with Jack Rogers and myself, honorary, made extremely short work of the parcel.

Shade follows sunshine. There was no amelioration of the accustomed fare at dinner; but a decided cloud on Mrs. Glumper's haughty brow was interpreted favourably by Jack—a close observer of human nature—as evincing her disgust at the costly reform to which she saw herself committed.

Alas! for once, our leader was wrong. Not that day, nor the following day, nor any other day, so long as that establishment survived, was there any departure from the time-(dis)honoured rules of diet.

It was long before I came into possession of the state papers actually exchanged on this occasion. Premising that my father, busied with his other letters, had handed over mine to my mother, saying, "Do see to this, my dear," here they are:

The Lady Caroline Trelawny to Mrs. Glumper.

"Dear Mrs. Glumper,—I trust that the size of the parcel I forward to my boy, will not alarm you. Charley is growing very rapidly, so rapidly, indeed, that his father drew my attention to the circumstance, not without some misgiving that he might outgrow his strength. You may smile at the anxiety that prompts me to remind one so experienced as yourself in the care of youth, that good, clean, and sufficient food is more than ever necessary to my tall boy. He is not a dainty boy, and the conditions I have mentioned will, I am sure, meet all that he, or I, on his behalf, could desire. With compliments to Dr. Glumper, I am, dear Mrs. Glumper, sincerely yours,
"CAROLINE M. TRELAWNY."

Mrs. Glumper to the Lady Caroline Trelawny.

"Dear Madam,—Perhaps the most satisfactory answer I can make to your obliging note will be conveyed in the assurance that Dr. Glumper, myself, our family, and the masters (except Monsieur Legourmet, who insists on providing his own meals), live invariably with, and as, our boys; and that, in the matter of food, there is neither stint nor compulsion.
"Respectfully yours,
"JEZEBEL GLUMPER."

There was, unfortunately, just sufficient colouring of truth in this to satisfy the consciences of both ladies. They *did* dine, or rather sit down, with us, and being helped first to the tit-bits, accompanied with hot gravy and et cæteras, at their own cross-table, got on pretty well. As for the good old doctor, he was the most innocent of accomplices in promoting our starvation. He simply did as his wife decreed, caring nothing for himself, and would have starved with his boys without a murmur.

After it became apparent that our move had failed, all, before the arrival of the fatal day, passed with me like a curious dream. I felt as if I no longer belonged to the school, hardly to myself, and though no verbal reference was made to my impending disappearance, I saw that no one had forgotten it. Significant were the facts, that Percy Pobjoy, who had owed me eightpence from time immemorial, borrowed that sum to repay me; and that another chap, with whom I had had a row, spontaneously asked my pardon.

Saturday—*the* day—appeared in due course. There remained but one more meal, one more chance for Mrs. Glumper and for me.

"If she gives us but a commonly decent feed to-day," muttered Jack Rogers, pinching my elbow, as we went in, "by Jove, Charley, my boy, we'll stop *your* nefarious plans!"

No such chance. There it was, the flabby mass of rice, helped first, as a good appetite-choking stuff, to relieve the succeeding dish from any undue pressure.

After rice appeared the much-dreaded pie, glaring yellowly, with its coarse pretentious outside—prototype of many a living humbug—veiling one knows not what of false and vile. O, the contrast to the rich and delicate article—alike only in name—sent by my mother!

The pie was served, and was undergoing the usual suspicious scrutiny, when Mrs. Glumper, with the voice of a herald, proclaimed:

"Master Trelawny will eat every grain of that rice before he receives anything further."

There was a half-audible titter; but I remained firm, and thus ended the last "dinner" at Glumper House.

Jack Rogers put his arm in mine.

"I'm sorry for this, Trelawny," he said.

"I'm *not*," said I, trying to smile, "exc—except for——" I thought of my mother, and broke down.

"We'll have a Palaver, at all events," said Jack.

In a moment, a large concourse assembled under our favourite elm. If the truth must out, I could have dispensed with this ceremony, which somehow imparted a sensation of being present at one's own burial. But Jack Rogers was not to be denied this splendid opportunity of speech-making.

He did speak, in a manner, and at a length, that must have been remembered in the school long after I—its theme—was forgotten there. In his peroration, he observed that the honour and the well-being of Glumper's could not, in this extremity, have been confided to worthier hands. Nor was it this community alone that was to profit by the important step about to be taken. The eyes of every school in Europe were, or would be, if they knew what was going on, fixed on Glumper House. Mr. Trelawny was about to place his foot on the first rung of the ladder of affluence, fame, and power. What pecuniary means, he would frankly ask, were at my disposal? I replied, with the like openness, "Eight-pence,"

"The precise amount," resumed Jack, triumphantly, "(within one and tenpence) from whence colossal fortunes spring! 'He began his immortal career with half-a-crown.' Or, 'The origin of this eminent citizen was of the humblest; he commenced life with two-and-six-pence.' Or, 'Our modern Crœsus began the battle of life with the moiety of a five-shilling piece. He died worth TWO MILLIONS sterling!' Such, are among our most familiar passages in biography. Charles, my boy, again you are in luck." And he shook my hand warmly.

I ventured incidentally to suggest that I was *not* in possession of the magical amount required.

"Nay, by George, but you shall be!" exclaimed Jack. "Here's sixpence towards it. Think of it when you're a confoundedly crusty old million-naire, and send old Jack a haunch from one of your deer-parks—the Scotch one. Who'll sub-scribe to the Trelawny Testimonial?"

Hard up as the good chaps were, so many came forward, that a sum of about nine-and-sixpence was poured into the hands of our chief. But Jack's remark had been working strangely in my mind. Something admonished me to keep strictly to the rule which had, apparently, prospered so well.

In a few words I thanked my mates, therefore, for their kind intentions, but declined to take more than was required to make up the exact fortune-making sum. I would do nothing (I added, in substance) to risk a failure, nor impair the innate vigour, the youthful freshness, of half-a-crown, by dabbling with an adolescent amount like ten-and-twopence: a sum entirely unas-sociated with any of those encouraging biogra-phies quoted by our president. I would take my half-crown—no more.

As the day was waning, it became necessary to make preparations for my departure. Accord-ingly, attended by a few faithful friends, I pro-ceeded to make up a small bundle, such as I could conveniently carry, leaving the remainder of my possessions at the disposal of fate. There was one thing I was very loth to abandon. It was a flower-pot, containing the commencement of a very promising scarlet-runner. It had been the source of great interest and consolation. I half resolved to make it the sharer of my fortunes. But Jack Rogers objected. In vain he taxed his memory to recal any one instance in which the successful adventurer had flung himself upon the world with half-a-crown *and* a scarlet-runner. If the case of Jack and the Beanstalk were relied upon, he (Rogers) would only remark that the present age of inquiry had succeeded in throwing very considerable doubt upon portions of that narrative. This was enough.

About escaping, there was no difficulty. Part of the playing-field was out of sight of the house, and, although it was penal to frequent this por-tion, and it was the duty of the monitor of the day to report any one so doing, on the present occasion the monitor in person gave me a leg up the wall. There was a last shaking of hands, and a suppressed cheer, when I paused for a moment on the top.

"You'll write that letter to-morrow, then, from—from somewhere?" said Jack, mysteriously. (I nodded.) "All right, old boy?"

"Ye-es," I responded. "All right, you know. Hoor——"

Down I dropped——adrift!

That wall seemed to make all the difference. I don't think that, until my feet alighted on the alien ground of Mr. Turfitt's brick-field, I had fully realised the fact of running away. But a runaway I was now; and, to do my boyish courage justice, no thought of returning or seeking the protection of home, ever entered into my imagination. One brief and bitter pang I did experience, as I thought of the probable effect the tidings of my flight might have upon the happy home circle; but I met it with the reflection that the letter I should write must set them at ease as to my personal safety and prospects. In the mean time, it was obviously desirable to get away.

Dr. Glumper's was situated in an open suburb north of London, and therefore, well on the high road to fortune. I set my face straight towards the quarter in which I concluded the City to lie, and trudged on, vaguely wondering what would happen to me when bedtime came.

Suddenly, a bright thought, suggested by the name on a public-house sign, shot across my mind. I had a friend—Philip Concanen—who resided at Chelsea, nothing of a walk, five miles. Phil had long outgrown Glumper's, though his name and his fame and a very rudely-executed miniature of Mrs. G., carved on the inside of his whilom desk, still survived. He was a middle-aged man now—going on, I should think, for nineteen—and had called once at Glumper's in a gig, driving himself. I had been a favourite of Phil's, and felt convinced that he would not only afford me his counsel, but keep *mine*. Well over the first steps of my pilgrimage, I had no fears about the remainder.

Philip was already in business with his father and uncle—wealthy brewers and distillers—whose establishment displayed on its river-face a frontage so imposing as almost to justify the tradition that it had once been mistaken for Chelsea Hospital. On the land side, you merely dived down a dark and narrow lane, sole shaft to the gold mine that lay beyond. Down this passage, as evening fell, I groped my way, and, by great good luck, found Philip in sole command (till Monday morning) of "Concanen Brothers, and Concanen."

Philip gave me a cordial welcome, and, thanks to his old housekeeper, a most heart-reviving supper, and listened to my story with all the kindness and interest I had expected; also with a degree of gravity I had *not* expected. Intercourse with men and vats had already taken off the edge of his romance. There is, in beer, a decided tendency to sap the life of sentiment. In meal, I have since observed, a contrary rule prevails. Your miller's daughter—if he has one —is almost always a heroine.

My friend criticised with some severity the golden visions of Jack Rogers, repudiated belief in the efficacy of half-a-crown as the especial keystone of affluence, and even hinted (though remotely) at the desirability of my making terms with the home authorities, and abandoning my enterprise.

On this point, however, I was firmness itself and after a lengthened discussion the following convention was agreed to:

That the old housekeeper, Mrs. Swigsby, should be admitted to our complete confidence, with a view to my occupancy of the spare bed-room till Monday. That on that day I should transfer my quarters to Philip's own private smoko-harness room, from whence a side portal and a passage, dark at noon, gave upon Paradise-alley, and thence to the privacy of Jew's-road. That I should retain such refuge until I had enjoyed an opportunity of "feeling my way"— which, indeed, would necessarily occur whenever I crossed the threshold. That on the slightest suspicion of my whereabout becoming known, I should depart, so as to avoid compromising my friend. Lastly, that I should at once write to my parents an assurance of my personal safety.

With some difficulty—owing to Mrs. Swigsby's being a deafer human creature than I could have conceived possible—that excellent lady was indoctrinated in the matter, and dismissing from her mind a first idea that I was the nephew of Mr. Arthur Thistlewood, and deeply compromised in certain, then recent, proceedings in Cato-street, promised every assistance. This arranged, I sat down to my letter:

"'My dear Papa and Mama,—I hope you are quite well. We ate up the Pie and other Things you so kindly sent, and then began Starving again. Rice, and Catterpillars, and what they call Beefstake-Pie but Isn't, *as usual*. I hoped you would have written to Mrs. Glumper, but perhaps you were Afrade. We held a Counsel, and Settled to run away One by One—till the Dinners get better. We drew Lots, and it Fell to me. I knew you would Aprove, for I heard you once say, about Captain Shurker, that it wasn't honourable to Back Out. I have my Second-best suit, some linen, my Bible, and Latin Delectus, and a Sum of Money which is the Beginning of a Fortune. I know what I am Doing—that is, I shall To-morrow—so I hope you won't be angry and kiss Mama and my love to Agnes and I am your Afectionate Dutiful Son,

"C. S. TRELAWNY."

Early on Monday morning, Phil introduced me to my new quarters in the smoko-harness room, where we found Mrs. Swigsby engaged in constructing what she called a "trumpery" bed. From the good lady's demeanour, I could not help fancying that she even now harboured some misgivings concerning me, for she glanced at me now and then as if she expected me to go off like a grenade. It was useless, however, to attempt to enlighten her further. Phil confessed as much, and owned that we must take our chance.

He introduced me to the dark passage and private entrance, and presenting me with the key, took his leave, assuring me that no one would enter the apartment until evening, when he would himself bring me supper, bear me company at that meal, and hear how I had felt my way.

When, a few minutes later, I turned into Jew's-road, the sensation of not belonging to myself came back rather strongly, bringing with it a brother sensation, still less soothing—that of not, for the moment, belonging to anybody else! Nevertheless, I held up my head, and marched on as confidently as if I expected an influential friend to meet me by appointment at the next corner.

How—*how* did people begin? Usually, I thought, with some happy incident. Would any obliging infant, of high birth, do me the favour to be nearly run over? Any stout gentleman—victim to casual orange-peel—trip and be picked up by me? Any hurrying man of commerce let fall a book containing securities of inestimable value, close to my feet? No; most of these things had had their turn. Fortune scorns to repeat herself. I had a conviction that I must begin at the foot of the ladder. "He" (some great man) "once swept a barber's shop," was a legend of my childhood. Where was such a barber?

"Wanted, a Lad."

It came like an answer. Were these characters *real?* If so, Fortune—though she writes an indifferent hand—has not deserted me. *I* am a lad. And wanted. Behold me!

I entered the establishment. It wasn't a barber's. Greasier. Pigs' toes, I imagine, prevailed. "What can I do for *you,* young gentleman?" inquired the stout white-aproned proprietor, brandishing an immense knife.

"Please, do you want a lad?" I asked.

The man looked at me from head to foot. Then he said:

"We *did,* but unfortnetly we only takes six parlour-boarders at a time; and the Markiss o' Queerfinch has just grabbed the last wacancy for his seventeenth son."

"I—I want to be a lad, sir," I faltered.

"Lookee here, young gentleman; if you don't want none of *my* trotters, use your own, or you'll get *me* into a scrape as well as yourself. Now, off with you!"

Twice more, tempted by similar announcements, I ventured to prefer my claims, but with no better success. One glance at my exterior seemed to satisfy everybody that I was not the lad for *them.* Yes, I was too smart! The recent runaway was visible in my still glossy blue jacket and gilt buttons; not to mention the snowy turn-down. I was not sorry when evening came, that I might return home, and recount my adventures to the sympathising Phil.

Philip agreed that I was *not,* perhaps, exactly the sort of messenger a struggling tripe-seller would select, but suggested that I might fly at

higher game. Why not feel my way among classes to whom a gentlemanly appearance and manner did *not* form an insuperable objection? Why not, indeed? Time was precious. Mrs. Swigsby's misgivings were evidently on the increase. I would do it to-morrow.

"Right, my boy," said Phil, as he bade me good night. "Straight, now, to the fountain head, you know."

I *didn't* exactly know. Feeling one's way, and going to the fountain head—though admirable as general principles—were, not so easy of application. Where *was* the fountain head?

"In your great banking and commercial firms," Phil had said, over our wine; "always deal with Principals."

My friend evidently assumed that I should seek out parties of this description. Accordingly, selecting from the Directory the names of a very eminent City banking firm, I "felt my way" towards their distant domicile, and found myself in the presence of about fifty clerks—all busily employed. After standing for some time unnoticed, I approached one of the desks.

"Please, sir, I want your head."

"My *what?*" inquired the clerk, with considerable energy. "What do you want with my head?"

I explained that I meant his Principal; the head of the firm : whereupon the clerk smiled languidly.

"Mr. Ingott's down at Goldborough Park," he said, "but if it's anything about the Turkish Loan, we'll send an express. He can be here to-morrow."

I assured him it had nothing to do with the Turkish Loan, or any loan, and that any other partner of the house would do as well.

The clerk nodded, whispered to another clerk and desiring me to follow, led the way through a labyrinth of desks, into an inner room, where sat an old gentleman reading the paper. He looked at me inquiringly through his gold eye-glasses. The clerk whispered—and—

"Well, my young friend?" said the old banker.

"Pl—please, sir," I blurted out, "do you want a confidential lad?"

The clerk tittered; but the old gentleman, with one look, dismissed him, and proceeded:

"Who sent you hither, my boy, and what do you mean?"

His manner was very kind, so I told him at once, that nobody sent me; that, acting upon advice, I was engaged in feeling my way, and wished to begin by being a lad—a *confidential* lad, if possible; that, with that view, I had come straight to the fountain head; that, being, I must confess, at variance with my friends, I could not mention whence I came, but that he might rely upon my honesty; and that I was prepared, if necessary, to deposit in the hands of the firm a certain sum of money, as an indemnification for any losses that might be incurred through my inexperience.

The old gentleman inquired the amount.

"Two-and-sixpence."

I saw his eye twinkle; then, as if a sudden thought had struck him, he put his hand upon my shoulder and turned me to the light. "Hem—I thought so," I fancied I heard him mutter. Then he added aloud: "See here, my lad. I cannot make so important an engagement on my own responsibility. I must consult my partners in the firm. Sit down in the messenger's room—that door yonder. In half an hour I will give you your answer."

In the messenger's room I found a respectable-looking youth, eating bread-and-cheese. He offered me some, but I could not eat. Kind as the old gentleman's manner was, there was something in it that gave me uneasiness. It almost seemed as if he knew me.

"Who," I asked the messenger, "is that old gentleman who said he must consult his partners?"

"Sir Edward Goldshore—him that lives at Bilton Abbey, near Penrhyn."

"Penrhyn? General Trelawny's?"

"That, sir, is the ticket. The general often lunches here when he's in town. Consult his partners, did the governor say? Why, they're all out of town but him!"

"Don't you," I asked, faintly, "think this room of yours rather hot? I'll—take a run—and—and come back before I'm wanted."

Ere the youth could start any objections I had vanished.

That unlucky day was doomed to an unluckier close. Concanen made his appearance in the harness-room with a somewhat harassed face.

"It's a bore, my dear old fellow, but I fear your camp must be broken up. There's no trusting old Swigsby. You must move on, Charley, my boy, and, if you won't go slick home, like a reasonable chap, feel your way in other quarters."

There was, obviously, no alternative. I marched on the following morning. But Phil's good offices did not cease until he had seen me established in a (very humble) lodging not far distant, but in a locality where I could continue to feel my way without much chance of recognition. The rent—five shillings a week—Phil at first insisted on paying; but, on my representation that the acceptance of any money aid might vitiate my entire future, the kind fellow consented to purchase, at full value, such articles of my wardrobe as would supply me with all that was necessary for an entire week, leaving my half-crown still intact.

Thus was I, for the second time, adrift. Fortune kept steadily aloof. Go whither, ask whom, I would, the same suspicious look invariably greeted me. Whether I brushed my jacket neatly, or tore experimental holes in the elbows, it seemed that I could never hit the desired medium between gentility and vagabondism.

I shall not describe at length those miserable days, nor the steady diminution of my hopes and resources, until the middle of the second week found me, with my rent paid, indeed, but destitute of everything save the clothes I stood in, and *sixpence!*

I had given up in despair all search for employment. Go home I would not. Of Phil I had heard nothing, and I feared to compromise him by any overt communication. What was to be done?

One morning, I was prowling feebly about, *very* hungry, and, every now and then, feeling the sixpence in my jacket-pocket, as though the very sight of a cook-shop might have drawn it forth, when I noticed an old Jew seated on the lower steps of a house. He was not a neat or a well-washed Jew. I don't think that I ever in after life beheld a dirtier; but my attention was drawn to him by the demeanour of a potboy, who, in passing, had muttered, "Old chap's sewn up!" and whistled on two fingers, almost over the man's head, a pæan of congratulation upon the circumstance.

The old Jew looked faintly up. The face, though grimy, was not, I thought, ignoble; and, indifferent whither I strolled, I turned to take another look at him. He was very old, very ragged, and, to all appearance, famine-stricken; at least, I never saw hunger written so legibly in any face, except my own. He made a languid motion with his fingers towards me, like a dying creature, but did not beg, and I passed on my way. Suddenly, the thought shot across me, "Should the old man *die!*"

The sixpence seemed to give a spontaneous leap in my pocket, as though inspired with the same idea. Back I went, wavering, for, if I yielded to charitable impulse, what must I myself do? If he would divide it with me—but how ask a dying man for change? I passed him again.

Either my fancy misled me, or the sixpence gave me a discontented punch in the side. "*But,*" I answered, as though in remonstrance with it, "you, are the last hope of my fortune; in giving *you*, I part with millions—'two millions.'" A last emphatic punch determined me. I turned once more, walked hastily back, and dropped my two millions into the old man's hand!

How I got through the remainder of that day I hardly know. It was about dusk, when, growing every moment more faint and desponding, I turned to crawl homeward. I was pausing unconsciously before a baker's window, when a hand touched my shoulder. It was my Jew. The old man had changed considerably for the better, and now, of the two, looked far the more alive.

"Good rolls those," said the old Jew, approvingly. "Hungry?"

Almost too weary to speak, I nodded.

"And—and—no money?" asked the old man, with curious eagerness.

I shook my head, and prepared to move away.

"I—I spent that sixpence," resumed the Jew, "but if you don't despise a poor man's haunt, I'll give you a supper, and, if you need it, lodging too. My castle is close at hand."

I looked at him with surprise, and followed him. Falling into a sort of mendicant gait, he shuffled feebly on, and, turning into a dark narrow street, composed of very small tenements indeed, paused at one of the nearest, and struck upon the window-sill with his crutch-stick.

"Take hold of my coat when she opens the door," said the old Jew. "You may find it darkish below."

It *was* darkish, insomuch that the "she" who opened to us was invisible in the gloom, but a silver voice, that was not the Jew's, uttered an exclamation of welcome, and died away, like a spirit's, into some upper region, whither we stumbled in pursuit. A candle-end, dimly flickering in the corner, revealed our conductress in the person of a girl of about fifteen, attired in a thick white robe which covered her from neck to foot, and seemed, so far as I might presume to judge, to be her only garment. The large sleeves were turned back to the elbows, as if she had been engaged in household work, and the inaudibility of her movements was accounted for by her feet being bare. A broad white fillet tied back immense masses of dark brown hair. The face! Boy as I was, and a] very sleepy and exhausted one—I was roused at once into a state of stupid ecstasy by one glance at her marvellous beauty. "Is it a woman? Is it a woman?" I remember gasping, as it were, to myself. And as she stood, for a few seconds, motionless, her form and dress like sculpture, her white arms extended towards me in questioning surprise, I felt as if it would be no sin to fall at her feet, in adoration of what seemed more of Heaven than earth.

"Supper, Zell," said the old Jew, and darkness fell upon the scene. Zell had vanished.

The rest of that evening was a blank, with passing gleams of Paradise. Fatigue and inanition forced me to sleep, even while striving to eat. But, in those intervals of glory, I was conscious of sitting at a feast, between the Queen of the Fairies, and an exceedingly ragged old Hebrew whom she addressed as grandfather; sensible that the latter (speaking as though I had been absent) told the former a story about me and a sixpence, which seemed to be amusing; aware, finally, that Queen Titania remarked, in a pitying voice:

"The child! He ought to be in bed!" And, without further ceremony, put me there.

My couch was on the floor of that same apartment, and the last thing I remember was Titania's foot, so small, so purely white, so bluely veined, withal so near my lips, that I would have kissed it, if I dared—but went to sleepwhile thinking of it.

My rest was so profound, that, when I awoke to another day, Zell and her grandfather were finishing breakfast. Both were dressed as on the preceding day; the old man, with his squalid aspect, tattered garments, and rusty shoes, offering a strange contrast to the bewitching creature, fresh and sweet as a dewy moss-rose, who sat beside him. If her beauty had asserted itself in the semi-darkness overnight, the full light of day only confirmed it more. The countenance was unquestionably of the Jewish order, but of the richest tint, the most refined and delicate mould. I lay in a sort of joyful stupor, utterly unable to remove my eyes from the glorious object. If love were ever born at eleven years old, here was the nativity of a passion that could never die. O, angel!— Zell suddenly discovered that I was awake.

After bringing me some tea, she quitted the room, and the old man came and sat down beside me. Having questioned me about my home and friends—to which I candidly replied that I had, at present, none to speak of, being engaged in simply feeling my way—he went on:

"You have been frank with me, my boy. I'll be frank with *you*. Though a very poor, poor man—oh, a *very* poor man—I am not, as you supposed, a beggar. I have means of living, such as they are, but these compel me to be much from home. My granddaughter, my Zell (what fool gave her that name I know not; she is called Zeruiah), has neither relation nor friend. For reasons I cannot now explain, she never quits this house. My heart bleeds at the solitude to which I am forced to condemn her. Stay with us, child, for a while. You shall have board and lodging, it may be some trifle over, when times are good. You can go on messages for Zell, and help her in the house. What say you?"

If the old gentleman had intimated that the reversion of the crown of England awaited my acceptance, my heart would have throbbed with far less exultant joy! *Stay* with her! See her! Serve her! Be her blessed thrall!

What I replied, I know not. I only know that ten minutes later the old gentleman had shuffled forth, and I, washing teacups under the eye of my beautiful mistress, had broken one, and received a box on the ear, delivered without any ceremony whatever. Zell was evidently as impulsive as she was beautiful. Presuming on her immense seniority of four years, the young lady made no more account of me than if I had been a kitten.

The room we sat in, and a little nook above, where Zell slept, were, like herself, scrupulously clean: all the remainder of the mansion being apparently given fairly over to decay and dirt. Our slender meals were prepared in the sitting-room, and provided from a daily sum, of I should think about fourpence-halfpenny, doled out by the lord of the mansion before leaving. My lady would instruct me where and how to invest this capital to the greatest advantage, and, according to my success, reward me on my return with a radiant smile, or a sounding box on the ear.

Mistress Zell seldom making me the recipient of her thoughts and words, it was by slow degrees that I learned the following particulars: That my host, Mr. Moses Jeremiah Abrahams, was a gentleman of habits so penurious, that he might have rivalled, if not eclipsed, the most illustrious misers of the age, had he only possessed anything to hoard. That Zell was dressed as I beheld her, to preclude the possibility of her going forth —to incur expenses—in the public ways. (As, sitting on the ground, while she told me this, I looked up in my lady's glorious eyes, it struck me that the old man might have had a tenderer reason.) That Mr. Abrahams, absent, most days, till dark, was, on certain days, later still. Finally, that I must not be surprised if, on one or more of those days, I heard his signal on the window-sill, but not himself on the stairs. "And *woe* to you!" concluded my lady, threatening me with her little hand, "if you betray our secret!"

"Our!" My heart turned faint, I caught her meaning instantly, and experienced the first burning touch of jealousy. My mistress had a lover.

"What makes you colour so, you stupid foolish boy?" said my lady, half laughing, half angry. "Can we trust you, or can we *not?*"

I stammered some nonsense about being at her command, body and soul. And I have no doubt I meant it.

My devotion was soon tested. That very evening (one of Mr. Abrahams' late ones) a knock, like his, sounded on the window-sill. Zell, bidding me follow, flew down stairs, and, softly opening the window, was clasped in the embrace of an individual to all appearance as ragged and infirm of mien as her grandfather himself.

For a moment she suffered this, then drew back, leaving the visitor her hand, which that monster, whoever he was, seemed to devour with kisses. There ensued a whispered conversation, during which I observed the speakers referred to me. Then, as if alarmed by a signal from without, the stranger vanished. We returned up-stairs.

Next morning my mistress gave me a note without address. I was to take it to a particular shop, and give it to a particular stranger who would accost me. No particular stranger was there. Afraid to return without fulfilling my mission, I was lingering over some trifling purchase, when a phaeton dashed up to the door, and a gentleman entered the shop. He was very handsome, wore thick black moustaches carefully curled, had long gilt spurs, and looked like an officer. He was well known to the shop-people, for he tossed about a number of articles, laughing and jesting with the mistress, but purchased nothing. Could *this* be my man? I managed, at all events, to let him see what I was carrying. We left the shop together.

"Toss it over! Quick, my lad!" said the gentleman, sharply. "Take this, and *this*" (he gave me another note, and half-a-crown). "And meet me here to-morrow."

I told him I did not want his money, but would take his note. He looked at me, uttered a long low whistle—expressive, I take it, of astonishment—and drove away.

The joy in my sweet mistress's eyes, and a white hand stroking my curls, even while she read the letter, were a sufficient reward. Then she made me her confidant. Her suitor was Lord John Loveless, son of the proud Earl of St. Buryans, with whom, owing to some little financial misunderstanding, poor Lord John was, for the moment, on terms so far from satisfactory, as to render it improbable that the earl would

yield anything like a cordial assent to his son's union with the granddaughter of an impoverished Jew. Hence the necessity for those clandestine interviews, which my mistress atoned for to her conscience, by sternly forbidding her lover ever to cross the threshold.

My lord was at the shop next morning as soon as I.

He took me familiarly by the arm.

"Come and take a pull on the river, boy. I want to have a talk with you."

It was not far to the river. We got a boat, and pulled off, my companion chatting pleasantly enough. At last he said:

"That old governor of yours keeps you pretty short, I take it? What does he do, now, with his money? Do you never hear him counting his guineas? Come!"

I positively denied it, and gave such candid reasons for my conviction that he was all but a pauper, that my companion seemed staggered. He became grave, not to say morose, and the row home seemed to bore him. I did not report to my lady all that had passed between us; I could not have left out his bad spirits when I described to him her poverty, and that might have pained her.

After this, my lord's visits became less frequent, and my mistress's smiles rarer. She moved about with a slower and a sadder step; and sometimes sat with her marble arms crossed on her lap, until I almost doubted if she lived. At which times, I would creep into the field of her eye, if but to change its fixed expression.

A terrible event came to rouse her. The old gentleman was brought home, one night, dying. He had been hustled, knocked down, and robbed, by some miscreants in the street. Though he had sustained no injury that should ordinarily prove mortal, the shock to his system, and, still more, the alleged robbery to which he perpetually referred, combined to give him to the grave. In spite of medical efforts he sank fast, and, at midnight, died.

My mistress, who had never left his side, bore all with a strange patience. I never saw her weep, but her white face and gleaming eyes struck me with awe.

A will, duly executed, was found, in which the old man, in general terms, bequeathed to his granddaughter, Zeruiah Abrahams, everything of which he should die possessed, appointing one Lemuel Samuelson guardian and executor. What money the old man had about him, when robbed, was never known. All the coin in the house amounted to no more than sufficed to pay the medical attendant, while the furniture was probably not worth more than twenty or thirty pounds. Part of this, with the assistance of a neighbour, we sold, to spare the old man a pauper's funeral; the rest, we thought, would provide clothes for Zell (since we must *both* now go out and feel our way), and support us both until we found our way. When this was done, the house looked desolate and wretched enough, and my poor mistress scarcely less so. Though she never spoke of it, the desertion of her lover—of whom in all that distressful time we never heard—cut her to the heart's core.

One day, before her clothes came, as I was moving restlessly about the room, thinking what I could say to comfort her, she suddenly lifted her head:

"Charley, will *you* desert me, too?"

"Zell! '*Desert* you!'" Like a young fool, as I was, I burst into a passion of tears.

"Don't—don't! My dear child—my good ch——!" And, infected by my tears, poor Zell laid her head on the table and wept aloud.'

Almost at that moment my eye was caught by an urchin in the street, beckoning eagerly. Stammering some excuse, I ran out.

"Gem' giv' me a bob," said the boy, "fur to say as he's a waitin' at the corner."

At the corner; or, more correctly, *round* it, stood Lord John Loveless.

"Now, my boy," said his lordship, very hurriedly, "I am here at great risk to—to myself, and have only a moment to stay. About your mistress? Is she well? Is she cared for? Did the old fellow *really* die a beggar?"

I replied, that the old gentleman had neither lived nor died a beggar, but that we had no money, and intended to feel our way towards work, as soon as we could go out.

Lord John seemed struck at this, and made an irresolute movement in the direction of the house.

"Won't you come in?" I forced myself to say.

"N—no," was the reply. "I can't. Urgent business elsewhere. See, boy. Give her this. Say I have been absent with my regiment, or I'd have sent before."

And, if ever noble gentleman skulked away, I think Lord John did.

Kneeling at my sweet mistress's feet, I faithfully recounted the interview. Zell listened, without once removing her eyes from mine. Then she said: "Put his—his wretched alms—into a cover, and take it to the address I shall write." All which was duly done,

But, the events of the day were not over. As we sat towards evening, discussing projects for the morrow, a stranger somewhat peremptorily demanded admittance, and, in company with another individual who had apparently been lurking aloof, produced some papers, and declared himself in possession of the house. He was our landlord. Our rent was deeply in arrear. His applications and threats having been alike disregarded by the eccentric Mr. Abrahams, he had taken the necessary steps to resume possession, and now came, inspired with an intense hatred (as he openly declared) for all Jew tenants, to enforce his rights.

It was in vain to remonstrate. We had not one shilling in our possession, and, for furniture, only our beds, chairs, table, and cooking utensils: all which, united, would not have paid half the debt.

"At least, sir," said my mistress, "you will not turn us into the streets, *to-night?*"

"Well!" said the fellow, reluctantly, "hardly *that*. But I'm up to these dodges, *I* promise you. Let you stay, and here you *will* stay. We'll stop that game. Without beds and window-sashes, you'll soon be ready to go. Collect the traps, Bill Bloxam, and look alive."

"It will soon be night, sir," said Zell, pale as a ghost: "a night that promises to be both cold and wet; in charity, leave us the protection of windows."

"Pin up your petticoat," returned the landlord, coolly. "*Here* she goes!"

He roughly tore at the window-sash. Out it came, crashing. But the rotten woodwork at the side, deprived of its support, and yielding as it seemed to some pressure from within, came away also. There was a heavy rushing fall that shook the very house—a rolling, ringing, spinning, settling down! From end to end, the apartment was literally carpeted with *gold!*

"Phsh!" said the reeling landlord, as he wiped the dust from his eyes.

My mistress was the first to recover composure. A watchman, on his way to night-duty, attracted by the crash, stood opposite. She bade me call him in, and, dismissing the now subdued landlord, procured a trusty guardian for the night. My mistress also despatched a special messenger in quest of Mr. Lemuel Samuelson, who, arriving with the dawn, joined us in further investigations.

Two thousand seven hundred guineas had been scattered on the floor. In different parts of the house, generally crammed into chinks and chasms of the decaying woodwork, were bank-notes to the amount of thirty-two thousand pounds. But even *that* was a trifle compared to the crafty old miser's foreign securities, which, disinterred in one lump, represented the immense sum of two hundred and ninety thousand pounds.

"And now, my love," said Mr. Samuelson, when both search and calculation were exhausted, "you will give Mrs. S. and me the pleasure of your company, at my little box at Sydenham, until you decide what *next* to do."

My mistress at once assented. Since the discovery of the treasure, she had had intervals of the deepest melancholy. Was she thinking what *might* have been, had the old man been less reticent? She had hardly addressed a word to me, and, until Mr. Samuelson came obsequiously to hand her to the carriage, I knew not if she would even bid me farewell. At last it was her guardian himself who drew her attention to me, by asking if she had any directions to give the "lad."

"The lad," repeated Zell, abstractedly.

"Call at my office, boy!" said Mr. Samuelson, who seemed impatient to get away. "By-the-by, what's your name?"

I made no answer. I was looking at my mistress.

"Sulky, eh?" said Mr. Samuelson. "Worse for *you*. Come, my love."

"Charley! Charley!" said Zell.

Then I *could* not answer. She waved her hand towards me, but her guardian led her away.

All that day, I sat at the window, as though I had fully expected her to return; but, in reality, I had no such idea. I knew that my darling mistress was gone—for ever, ever, gone—and had taken with her all joy, all happiness, all desire of life. I was conscious of a sense of hunger, but had no heart to look for food; at the time when we used to prepare our supper on those happy evenings, I crept to my lady's little bed, and lay down *there*. A curious rushing sound was in my ears, and my pulse seemed rather to give a continuous shudder, than to beat. Dreams came, without introductory ceremony of sleep. I heard myself shouting and struggling. Then, darkness . . . .

I awoke in my father's house. I had been there three weeks. Though very weak, I was in the path of recovery, and was soon in condition to return to school. But not to Glumper's. No.

I learned that, in my delirium, I had given a clue to my name and residence. What after-communications I made, I cannot say: I only know that both my mother, and my saucy little Agnes, were as familiar with the name of Zell as my own daily thoughts were. She was my love, my queen, my darling only mistress. In that faith, and in the firm assurance that I should one blessed day see her again, I grew to manhood.

There was a grand ball at Dublin Castle, at which I, a young lieutenant of dragoons, chanced to be present and abetting. The reception was more than usually crowded and magnificent, it being the farewell of a popular lord-lieutenant.

As the latter moved about among his smiling guests, he halted at a group beside me.

"Well, young gentlemen," said his excellency, "who is the successful knight? Surely this prize is not to escape us all! Resplendent beauty—sweetness — accomplishments — twelve thousand a year. Shame to Ireland, if this Mexican belle quits us to-night, her last in the land (for I hear she returns to Mexico), a disengaged woman!"

"She will *not*, my lord," replied Colonel Walsingham.

"Hah! Who wins?" asked his excellency, hardly less interested than if he had himself been a candidate.

"That is doubtful, still," put in young Lord Goring. "Hawkins, Rushton, O'Rourke, Walsingham, St. Buryans, my humble self, have all been 'mentioned' in the race. St. Buryans for choice."

"Why so?" asked his lordship.

"The lady has been seated this whole evening beside St. Buryans' lady-mother," said Goring, in a low voice. "And she's the cleverest woman, at a finish, in Christendom—or Jewry either."

"You said it would be decided to-night?"

"Thus. The young lady will dance but once, the last dance. We have all solicited the honour. She reserves her choice. It has been agreed to accept the augury. Your lordship understands? The unsuccessful withdraw."

His excellency nodded, smiled, and passed on.

A few minutes later, a movement in the room drew my attention. All eyes seemed directed towards one object. Up the centre of the room, leaning on the arm of Lord John Loveless, now Earl St. Buryans, was passing my beautiful mistress! Taller—fuller, no whit lovelier, for that could not be. She looked full in my face. I thought she paused for a second. No, the superb brown eyes were languidly withdrawn, and, without recognition, she moved on.

The last dance was announced from the orchestra. As if under a spell, I placed myself opposite to my lady's chair, though remote from it. I saw the rival suitors, with well-bred self-possession, gather round, and each in turn prefer his claim. All were declined. St. Buryans—by whose haughty-looking mother my lady sat—alone remained. He approached her with confidence, his mother greeting him with a victorious smile. Before he could open his lips, Zell rose:

"Give me your arm. I wish to cross the room," she said to him haughtily.

She *did* cross. She came to *me*. Drawing her arm away from her conductor's, she held out both her little hands.

"Charley, Charley! Don't you know me? I come to ask you to—to dance with me—with your old friend, Zell."

We have more than one deer park—but it was from the Scotch one that, on Zell's reminder (she always pretends to be older and more thoughtful than I), I sent my friend Jack Rogers a haunch worthy of a king's acceptance.

V.

ANOTHER PAST LODGER RELATES HIS OWN GHOST STORY.

The circumstances I am about to relate to you have truth to recommend them. They happened to myself, and my recollection of them is as vivid as if they had taken place only yesterday. Twenty years, however, have gone by since that night. During those twenty years I have told the story to but one other person. I tell it now with a reluctance which I find it difficult to overcome. All I entreat, meanwhile, is that you will abstain from forcing your own conclusions upon me. I want nothing explained away. I desire no arguments. My mind on this subject is quite made up, and, having the testimony of my own senses to rely upon, I prefer to abide by it.

Well! It was just twenty years ago, and within a day or two of the end of the grouse season. I had been out all day with my gun, and had had no sport to speak of. The wind was due east; the month, December; the place, a bleak wide moor in the far north of England. And I had lost my way. It was not a pleasant place in which to lose one's way, with the first feathery flakes of a coming snow-storm just fluttering down upon the heather, and the leaden evening closing in all around. I shaded my eyes with my hand, and stared anxiously into the gathering darkness, where the purple moorland melted into a range of low hills, some ten or twelve miles distant. Not the faintest smoke-wreath, not the tiniest cultivated patch, or fence, or sheep-track, met my eyes in any direction. There was nothing for it but to walk on, and take my chance of finding what shelter I could, by the way. So I shouldered my gun again, and pushed wearily forward; for I had been on foot since an hour after daybreak, and had eaten nothing since breakfast.

Meanwhile, the snow began to come down with ominous steadiness, and the wind fell. After this, the cold became more intense, and the night came rapidly up. As for me, my prospects darkened with the darkening sky, and my heart grew heavy as I thought how my young wife was already watching for me through the window of our little inn parlour, and thought of all the suffering in store for her throughout this weary night. We had been married four months, and, having spent our autumn in the Highlands, were now lodging in a remote little village situated just on the verge of the great English moorlands. We were very much in love, and, of course, very happy. This morning, when we parted, she had implored me to return before dusk, and I had promised her that I would. What would I not have given to have kept my word! Even now, weary as I was, I felt that with a supper, an hour's rest, and a guide, I might still get back to her before midnight, if only guide and shelter could be found.

And all this time, the snow fell and the night thickened. I stopped and shouted every now and then, but my shouts seemed only to make the silence deeper. Then a vague sense of uneasiness came upon me, and I began to remember stories of travellers who had walked on and on in the falling snow until, wearied out, they were fain to lie down and sleep their lives away. Would it be possible, I asked myself, to keep on thus through all the long dark night? Would there not come a time when my limbs must fail, and my resolution give way? When I, too, must sleep the sleep of death. Death! I shuddered. How hard to die just now, when life lay all so bright before me! How hard for my darling, whose whole loving heart——but that thought was not to be borne! To banish it, I shouted again, louder and longer, and then listened eagerly. Was my shout answered, or did I only fancy that I heard a far-off cry? I hallooed again, and again the echo followed. Then a wavering speck of light came suddenly out of the dark, shifting, disappearing, growing momentarily nearer and brighter. Running towards it at full speed, I found myself, to my great joy, face to face with an old man and a lantern.

"Thank God!" was the exclamation that burst involuntarily from my lips.

Blinking and frowning, he lifted his lantern and peered into my face.

"What for?" growled he, sulkily.

"Well—for you. I began to fear I should be lost in the snow."

"Eh, then, folks do get cast away hereabouts fra' time to time, an' what's to hinder you from bein' cast away ·likewise, if the Lord's so minded?"

"If the Lord is so minded that you and I shall be lost together, friend, we must submit," I replied; "but I don't mean to be lost without you. How far am I now from Dwolding?"

"A gude twenty mile, more or less."

"And the nearest village?"

"The nearest village is Wyke, an' that's twelve mile t'other side."

"Where do you live, then?"

"Out yonder," said he, with a vague jerk of the lantern.

"You're going home, I presume?"

"Maybe I am."

"Then I'm going with you."

The old man shook his head, and rubbed his nose reflectively with the handle of the lantern.

"It ain't o' no use," growled he. "He 'ont let you in—not he."

"We'll see about that," I replied, briskly. "Who is He?"

"The master."

"Who is the master?"

"That's nowt to you," was the unceremonious reply.

"Well, well; you lead the way, and I'll engage that the master shall give me shelter and a supper to-night."

"Eh, you can try him!" muttered my reluctant guide; and, still shaking his head, he hobbled, gnome-like, away through the falling snow. A large mass loomed up presently out of the darkness, and a huge dog rushed out, barking furiously.

"Is this the house?" I asked.

"Ay, it's the house. Down, Bey!" And he fumbled in his pocket for the key.

I drew up close behind him, prepared to lose no chance of entrance, and saw in the little circle of light shed by the lantern that the door was heavily studded with iron nails, like the door of a prison. In another minute he had turned the key and I had pushed past him into the house.

Once inside, I looked round with curiosity, and found myself in a great raftered hall, which served, apparently, a variety of uses. One end was piled to the roof with corn, like a barn. The other was stored with flour-sacks, agricultural implements, casks, and all kinds of miscellaneous lumber; while from the beams overhead hung rows of hams, flitches, and bunches of dried herbs for winter use. In the centre of the floor stood some huge object gauntly dressed in a dingy wrapping-cloth, and reaching half way to the rafters. Lifting a corner of this cloth, I saw, to my surprise, a telescope of very considerable size, mounted on a rude moveable platform with four small wheels. The tube was made of painted wood, bound round with bands of metal rudely fashioned; the speculum, so far as I could estimate its size in the dim light, measured at least fifteen inches in diameter. While I was yet examining the instrument, and asking myself whether it was not the work of some self-taught optician, a bell rang sharply.

"That's for you," said my guide, with a malicious grin. "Yonder's his room."

He pointed to a low black door at the opposite side of the hall. I crossed over, rapped somewhat loudly, and went in, without waiting for an invitation. A huge, white-haired old man rose from a table covered with books and papers, and confronted me sternly.

"Who are you?" said he. "How came you here? What do you want?"

"James Murray, barrister-at-law. On foot across the moor. Meat, drink, and sleep."

He bent his bushy brows into a portentous frown.

"Mine is not a house of entertainment," he said, haughtily. "Jacob, how dared you admit this stranger?"

"I didn't admit him," grumbled the old man. "He followed me over the muir, and shouldered his way in before me. I'm no match for six foot two."

"And pray, sir, by what right have you forced an entrance into my house?"

"The same by which I should have clung to your boat, if I were drowning. The right of self-preservation."

"Self-preservation?"

"There's an inch of snow on the ground already," I replied, briefly; "and it would be deep enough to cover my body before daybreak."

He strode to the window, pulled aside a heavy black curtain, and looked out.

"It is true," he said. "You can stay, if you choose, till morning. Jacob, serve the supper."

With this he waved me to a seat, resumed his own, and became at once absorbed in the studies from which I had disturbed him.

I placed my gun in a corner, drew a chair to the hearth, and examined my quarters at leisure. Smaller and less incongruous in its arrangements than the hall, this room contained, nevertheless, much to awaken my curiosity. The floor was carpetless. The whitewashed walls were in parts scrawled over with strange diagrams, and in others covered with shelves crowded with philosophical instruments, the uses of many of which were unknown to me. On one side of the fireplace, stood a bookcase filled with dingy folios; on the other, a small organ, fantastically decorated with painted carvings of mediæval saints and devils. Through the half-opened door of a cupboard at the further end of the room, I saw a long array of geological specimens, surgical preparations, crucibles, retorts, and jars of chemicals; while on the mantelshelf beside me, amid a number of small objects, stood a model of the solar system, a small galvanic battery, and a microscope. Every chair had its burden. Every corner was heaped high with books. The very floor was littered over with maps, casts, papers, tracings, and learned lumber of all conceivable kinds.

I stared about me with an amazement increased by every fresh object upon which my eyes chanced to rest. So strange a room I had never seen; yet seemed it stranger still, to find such a room in a lone farm-house amid those wild and solitary moors! Over and over again, I looked from my host to his surroundings, and from his surroundings back to my host, asking myself who and what he could be? His head was singularly fine; but it was more the head of a poet than of a philosopher. Broad in the temples, prominent over the eyes, and clothed with a rough profusion of perfectly white hair, it had all the ideality and much of the ruggedness that characterises the head of Louis von Beethoven. There were the same deep lines about the mouth, and the same stern furrows in the brow. There was the same concentration of expression. While I was yet observing him, the door opened, and Jacob brought in the supper. His master then closed his book, rose, and with more courtesy of manner than he had yet shown, invited me to the table.

A dish of ham and eggs, a loaf of brown bread, and a bottle of admirable sherry, were placed before me.

"I have but the homeliest farm-house fare to offer you, sir," said my entertainer. "Your appetite, I trust, will make up for the deficiencies of our larder."

I had already fallen upon the viands, and now protested, with the enthusiasm of a starving sportsman, that I had never eaten anything so delicious.

He bowed stiffly, and sat down to his own supper, which consisted, primitively, of a jug of milk and a basin of porridge. We ate in silence, and, when we had done, Jacob removed the tray. I then drew my chair back to the fireside. My host, somewhat to my surprise, did the same, and turning abruptly towards me, said:

"Sir, I have lived here in strict retirement for three-and-twenty years. During that time, I have not seen as many strange faces, and I have not read a single newspaper. You are the first stranger who has crossed my threshold for more than four years. Will you favour me with a few words of information respecting that outer world from which I have parted company so long?"

"Pray interrogate me," I replied. "I am heartily at your service."

He bent his head in acknowledgment; leaned forward, with his elbows resting on his knees and his chin supported in the palms of his hands; stared fixedly into the fire; and proceeded to question me.

His inquiries related chiefly to scientific matters, with the later progress of which, as applied to the practical purposes of life, he was almost wholly unacquainted. No student of science myself, I replied as well as my slight information permitted; but the task was far from easy, and I was much relieved when, passing from interrogation to discussion, he began pouring forth his own conclusions upon the facts which I had been attempting to place before him. He talked, and I listened spellbound. He talked till I believe he almost forgot my presence, and only thought aloud. I had never heard anything like it then; I have never heard anything like it since. Familiar with all systems of all philosophies, subtle in analysis, bold in generalisation, he poured forth his thoughts in an uninterrupted stream, and, still leaning forward in the same moody attitude with his eyes fixed upon the fire, wandered from topic to topic, from speculation to speculation, like an inspired dreamer. From practical science to mental philosophy; from electricity in the wire to electricity in the nerve; from Watts to Mesmer, from Mesmer to Reichenbach, from Reichenbach to Swedenborg, Spinoza, Condillac, Descartes, Berkeley, Aristotle, Plato, and the Magi and mystics of the East, were transitions which, however bewildering in their variety and scope, seemed easy and harmonious upon his lips as sequences in music. By-and-by—I forget now by what link of conjecture or illustration— he passed on to that field which lies beyond the boundary line of even conjectural philosophy, and reaches no man knows whither. He spoke of the soul and its aspirations; of the spirit and its powers; of second sight; of prophecy; of those phenomena which, under the names of ghosts, spectres, and supernatural appearances, have been denied by the sceptics and attested by the credulous, of all ages.

"The world," he said, "grows hourly more and more sceptical of all that lies beyond its own narrow radius; and our men of science foster the fatal tendency. They condemn as fable all that resists experiment. They reject as false all that cannot be brought to the test of the laboratory or the dissecting-room. Against what superstition have they waged so long and obstinate a war, as against the belief in apparitions? And yet what superstition has maintained its hold upon the minds of men so long and so firmly? Show me any fact in physics, in history, in archæology, which is supported by testimony so wide and so various. Attested by all races of men, in all ages, and in all climates, by the soberest sages of antiquity, by the rudest savage of to-day, by the Christian, the Pagan, the Pantheist, the Materialist, this phenomenon is treated as a nursery tale by the philosophers of our century. Circumstantial evidence weighs with them as a feather in the balance. The comparison of causes with effects, however valuable in physical science, is put aside as worthless and unreliable. The evidence of competent witnesses, however conclusive in a court of justice, counts for nothing. He who pauses before he pronounces, is condemned as a trifler. He who believes, is a dreamer or a fool."

He spoke with bitterness, and, having said thus, relapsed for some minutes into silence. Presently he raised his head from his hands, and added, with an altered voice and manner,

"I, sir, paused, investigated, believed, and was not ashamed to state my convictions to the world. I, too, was branded as a visionary, held up to ridicule by my contemporaries, and hooted from that field of science in which I had laboured

with honour during all the best years of my life. These things happened just three-and-twenty years ago. Since then, I have lived as you see me living now, and the world has forgotten me, as I have forgotten the world. You have my history."

"It is a very sad one," I murmured, scarcely knowing what to answer.

"It is a very common one," he replied. "I have only suffered for the truth, as many a better and wiser man has suffered before me."

He rose, as if desirous of ending the conversation, and went over to the window.

"It has ceased snowing," he observed, as he dropped the curtain, and came back to the fireside.

"Ceased!" I exclaimed, starting eagerly to my feet. "Oh, if it were only possible—but no! it is hopeless. Even if I could find my way across the moor, I could not walk twenty miles to-night."

"Walk twenty miles to-night!" repeated my host. "What are you thinking of?"

"Of my wife," I replied, impatiently. "Of my young wife, who does not know that I have lost my way, and who is at this moment breaking her heart with suspense and terror."

"Where is she?"

"At Dwolding, twenty miles away."

"At Dwolding," he echoed, thoughtfully. "Yes, the distance, it is true, is twenty miles; but—are you so very anxious to save the next six or eight hours?"

"So very, very anxious, that I would give ten guineas at this moment for a guide and a horse."

"Your wish can be gratified at a less costly rate," said he, smiling. "The night mail from the north, which changes horses at Dwolding, passes within five miles of this spot, and will be due at a certain cross-road in about an hour and a quarter. If Jacob were to go with you across the moor, and put you into the old coach-road, you could find your way, I suppose, to where it joins the new one?"

"Easily—gladly."

He smiled again, rang the bell, gave the old servant his directions, and, taking a bottle of whisky and a wine-glass from the cupboard in which he kept his chemicals, said:

"The snow lies deep, and it will be difficult walking to-night on the moor. A glass of usquebaugh before you start?"

I would have declined the spirit, but he pressed it on me, and I drank it. It went down my throat like liquid flame, and almost took my breath away.

"It is strong," he said; "but it will help to keep out the cold. And now you have no moments to spare. Good night!"

I thanked him for his hospitality, and would have shaken hands, but that he had turned away before I could finish my sentence. In another minute I had traversed the hall, Jacob had locked the outer door behind me, and we were out on the wide white moor.

Although the wind had fallen, it was still bitterly cold. Not a star glimmered in the black vault overhead. Not a sound, save the rapid crunching of the snow beneath our feet, disturbed the heavy stillness of the night. Jacob, not too well pleased with his mission, shambled on before in sullen silence, his lantern in his hand, and his shadow at his feet. I followed, with my gun over my shoulder, as little inclined for conversation as himself. My thoughts were full of my late host. His voice yet rang in my ears. His eloquence yet held my imagination captive. I remember to this day, with surprise, how my over-excited brain retained whole sentences and parts of sentences, troops of brilliant images, and fragments of splendid reasoning, in the very words in which he had uttered them. Musing thus over what I had heard, and striving to recal a lost link here and there, I strode on at the heels of my guide, absorbed and unobservant. Presently—at the end, as it seemed to me, of only a few minutes—he came to a sudden halt, and said:

"Yon's your road. Keep the stone fence to your right hand, and you can't fail of the way."

"This, then, is the old coach-road?"

"Ay, 'tis the old coach-road."

"And how far do I go, before I reach the cross-roads?"

"Nigh upon three mile."

I pulled out my purse, and he became more communicative.

"The road's a fair road enough," said he, "for foot passengers; but 'twas over steep and narrow for the northern traffic. You'll mind where the parapet's broken away, close again the sign-post. It's never been mended since the accident."

"What accident?"

"Eh, the night mail pitched right over into the valley below—a 'gude fifty feet an' more—just at the worst bit o' road in the whole county."

"Horrible! Were many lives lost?"

"All. Four were found dead, and t'other two died next morning."

"How long is it since this happened?"

"Just nine year."

"Near the sign-post, you say? I will bear it in mind. Good night."

"Gude night, sir, and thankee." Jacob pocketed his half-crown, made a faint pretence of touching his hat, and trudged back by the way he had come.

I watched the light of his lantern till it quite disappeared, and then turned to pursue my way alone. This was no longer matter of the slightest difficulty, for, despite the dead darkness overhead, the line of stone fence showed distinctly enough against the pale gleam of the snow. How silent it seemed now, with only my footsteps to listen to; how silent and how solitary! A strange disagreeable sense of loneliness stole over me. I walked faster. I hummed a fragment of a tune. I cast up enormous sums in my head, and accumulated them at compound interest. I did my best, in short, to forget the startling speculations to which I had but just been listening, and, to some extent, I succeeded.

Meanwhile the night air seemed to become colder and colder, and though I walked fast I found it impossible to keep myself warm. My feet were like ice. I lost sensation in my hands, and grasped my gun mechanically. I even breathed with difficulty, as though, instead of traversing a quiet north country highway, I were scaling the uppermost heights of some gigantic Alp. This last symptom became presently so distressing, that I was forced to stop for a few minutes, and lean against the stone fence. As I did so, I chanced to look back up the road, and there, to my infinite relief, I saw a distant point of light, like the gleam of an approaching lantern. I at first concluded that Jacob had retraced his steps and followed me; but even as the conjecture presented itself, a second light flashed into sight—a light evidently parallel with the first, and approaching at the same rate of motion. It needed no second thought to show me that these must be the carriage-lamps of some private vehicle, though it seemed strange that any private vehicle should take a road professedly disused and dangerous.

There could be no doubt, however, of the fact, for the lamps grew larger and brighter every moment, and I even fancied I could already see the dark outline of the carriage between them. It was coming up very fast, and quite noiselessly, the snow being nearly a foot deep under the wheels.

And now the body of the vehicle became distinctly visible behind the lamps. It looked strangely lofty. A sudden suspicion flashed upon me. Was it possible that I had passed the cross-roads in the dark without observing the sign-post, and could this be the very coach which I had come to meet?

No need to ask myself that question a second time, for here it came round the bend of the road, guard and driver, one outside passenger, and four steaming greys, all wrapped in a soft haze of light, through which the lamps blazed out, like a pair of fiery meteors.

I jumped forward, waved my hat, and shouted. The mail came down at full speed, and passed me. For a moment I feared that I had not been seen or heard, but it was only for a moment. The coachman pulled up; the guard, muffled to the eyes in capes and comforters, and apparently sound asleep in the rumble, neither answered my hail nor made the slightest effort to dismount; the outside passenger did not even turn his head. I opened the door for myself, and looked in. There were but three travellers inside, so I stepped in, shut the door, slipped into the vacant corner, and congratulated myself on my good fortune.

The atmosphere of the coach seemed, if possible, colder than that of the outer air, and was pervaded by a singularly damp and disagreeable smell. I looked round at my fellow-passengers. They were all three, men, and all silent. They did not seem to be asleep, but each leaned back in his corner of the vehicle, as if absorbed in his own reflections. I attempted to open a conversation.

"How intensely cold it is to-night," I said, addressing my opposite neighbour.

He lifted his head, looked at me, but made no reply.

"The winter," I added, "seems to have begun in earnest."

Although the corner in which he sat was so dim that I could distinguish none of his features very clearly, I saw that his eyes were still turned full upon me. And yet he answered never a word.

At any other time I should have felt, and perhaps expressed, some annoyance, but at the moment I felt too ill to do either. The icy coldness of the night air had struck a chill to my very marrow, and the strange smell inside the coach was affecting me with an intolerable nausea. I shivered from head to foot, and, turning to my left-hand neighbour, asked if he had any objection to an open window?

He neither spoke nor stirred.

I repeated the question somewhat more loudly, but with the same result. Then I lost patience, and let the sash down. As I did so, the leather strap broke in my hand, and I observed that the glass was covered with a thick coat of mildew, the accumulation, apparently, of years. My attention being thus drawn to the condition of the coach, I examined it more narrowly, and saw by the uncertain light of the outer lamps that it was in the last state of dilapidation. Every part of it was not only out of repair, but in a condition of decay. The sashes splintered at a touch. The leather fittings were crusted over with mould, and literally rotting from the woodwork. The floor was almost breaking away beneath my feet. The whole machine, in short, was foul with damp, and had evidently been dragged from some outhouse in which it had been mouldering away for years, to do another day or two of duty on the road.

I turned to the third passenger, whom I had not yet addressed, and hazarded one more remark.

"This coach," I said, "is in a deplorable condition. The regular mail, I suppose, is under repair?"

He moved his head slowly, and looked me in the face, without speaking a word. I shall never forget that look while I live. I turned cold at heart under it. I turn cold at heart even now when I recal it. His eyes glowed with a fiery unnatural lustre. His face was livid as the face of a corpse. His bloodless lips were drawn back as if in the agony of death, and showed the gleaming teeth between.

The words that I was about to utter died upon my lips, and a strange horror—a dreadful horror—came upon me. My sight had by this time become used to the gloom of the coach, and I could see with tolerable distinctness. I turned to my opposite neighbour. He, too, was looking at me, with the same startling pallor in his face, and the same stony glitter in his eyes. I passed my hand across my brow. I turned to the passenger on the seat beside my own, and saw—oh Heaven! how shall I describe what I saw? I saw that he was no living man—that none of them were living men, like myself! A pale phosphorescent light—the light of putrefaction—played upon their awful faces; upon their hair, dank with the dews of the grave; upon their clothes, earth-stained and dropping to pieces; upon their hands, which were as the hands of corpses long buried. Only their eyes, their terrible eyes, were living; and those eyes were all turned menacingly upon me!

A shriek of terror, a wild unintelligible cry for help and mercy, burst from my lips as I flung myself against the door, and strove in vain to open it.

In that single instant, brief and vivid as a landscape beheld in the flash of summer lightning, I saw the moon shining down through a rift of stormy cloud—the ghastly sign-post rearing its warning finger by the wayside—the broken parapet—the plunging horses—the black gulf below. Then, the coach reeled like a ship at sea. Then, came a mighty crash—a sense of crushing pain—and then, darkness.

It seemed as if years had gone by when I awoke one morning from a deep sleep, and found my wife watching by my bedside. I will pass over the scene that ensued, and give you, in half a dozen words, the tale she told me with tears of thanksgiving. I had fallen over a precipice, close against the junction of the old coach-road and the new, and had only been saved from certain death by lighting upon a deep snowdrift that had accumulated at the foot of the rock beneath. In this snowdrift I was discovered at daybreak, by a couple of shepherds, who carried me to the nearest shelter, and brought a surgeon to my aid. The surgeon found me in a state of raving delirium, with a broken arm and a compound fracture of the skull. The letters in my pocket-book showed my name and address; my wife was summoned to nurse me; and, thanks to youth and a fine constitution, I came out of danger at last. The place of my fall, I need scarcely say, was precisely that at which a frightful accident had happened to the north mail nine years before.

I never told my wife the fearful events which I have just related to you. I told the surgeon who attended me; but he treated the whole adventure as a mere dream born of the fever in my brain. We discussed the question over and over again, until we found that we could discuss it with temper no longer, and then we dropped it. Others may form what conclusions they please —I *know* that twenty years ago I was the fourth inside passenger in that Phantom Coach.

VI.

ANOTHER PAST LODGER RELATES
CERTAIN PASSAGES TO HER HUSBAND.

[INTRODUCTORY NOTE BY MAJOR JACKMAN. The country clergyman and his quiet and better than pretty wife, who occupied my respected friend's second floor for two spring months of four successive years, were objects of great interest, both with my respected friend and with me. One evening we took tea with them, and happened to speak of a pretty wilful-looking young creature and her husband—friends of theirs— who had dined with them on the previous day.

"Ah!" said the clergyman, taking his wife's hand very tenderly in his; "thereby hangs a tale. Tell it to our good friends, my dear." "I can address it, Owen," said his wife, hesitating, "to nobody but you." "Address it, then, to me, my darling," said he, "and Mrs. Lirriper and the Major will be none the worse listeners." So she went on as follows, with her hand resting in his all the time. Signed, J. JACKMAN.]

The first time I saw you again, after the years long and many which had passed over us since our childhood, I was watching for you on the peak of the hill, from whence I could see furthest down the steep and shady lane along which you were coming up to our hamlet from the plain below me. All day I had been anxious that when you arrived, our hills, which you must have forgotten, should put on their most gorgeous beauty; but now the sunset was come which would leave us the bare and grey outlines of the rocks only, and, from the kindling sky there fell bars of golden sunshine, with darker rays underlying them, slanting down the slopes of the mountain, and touching every rounded knoll and little dimpling dell with such a glory, that even the crimson and purple tints of the budding bilberry wires far away towards the level table-land where the summits blended, glowed, and burned under the farewell light. Just then there came a shout of welcome, like the shout of harvest-home, ringing up through the quiet air, and, straining my shaded eyes to catch the first glimpse, I saw you walking in the midst of a band of our sturdy, sunburnt villagers, with the same slight and delicate-looking frame, and pale, grave pleasant face, and shy and timid manner that were yours when we were boy and girl together.

Our little hamlet had gathered itself from time to time, without any special plan or purpose, upon one of the lower terraces of our cluster of mountains, separated from the nearest villages by a wide tract of land, only to be crossed by a steep, stony, deep-rutted lanes, overhung with wild hedgerows, and almost impassable in the winter. During the summer, when the faint tones of the bells of our parish church were borne up to us on the calm air, a little procession of us, the girls and children riding on rough hill-ponies, were wont to wind down the lanes to the Sunday morning service; but in winter no one thought of the pilgrimage, unless some of the young men had sweethearts in the village whom they hoped to meet at church. Mr. Vernon, the rector, being an archdeacon, hardly less than a bishop in dignity and importance, was deeply distressed at the heathenish darkness of his mountain district; and he and my father, who owned the great hill-farm, which gave employment to the people of our hamlet, at last built the little red-brick church, with no tower, and smaller than our barn, which stands upon the point of the mountain terrace, overlooking the great plain that stretches away from our feet up to the very far horizon.

There might have been a difficulty in finding a curate who would live up at Ratlinghope, with no other social intercourse than could be obtained by a long march into the peopled plain below us; but I knew afterwards that the church, so far as my father's share in it was concerned, had been built for you. You were just taking orders, and you had a pleasant remembrance of the large old rambling half-timber house where you had spent some months of your childhood; so when we wrote to you that your dwelling would be in our own house, your study being the blue parlour which looked down the green sheltered dell where the young lambs were folded, you answered that you would gladly take the charge, and live with us again on the sweet, free heathery uplands, where you had breathed in health and strength in your early boyhood.

You were grave and studious, and withal so simple-hearted, that the seclusion and the primitive manners of our hamlet made it a very Eden to you. You had never forgotten our old haunts, and we revisited them together, for in the first moment of our greeting you had fallen into your habit of dependence upon me, and of demanding my companionship, as when you were a delicate boy of six years, and I a strong, healthy, mountain girl three years older. To me only, could you utter your thoughts freely, for your natural shyness closed your lips to strangers; and all were strangers to you, even those who had known you for a lifetime, if they did not possess the touch of sympathy which your spirit needed before it would open its treasures. Up on the hill-side, when the steady noontide seemed as unchangeable as the everlasting rocks about us, or when the tremulous dusk stole with silent shadows over the fading headlands, you and I sat together, while I listened to the unreserved outpourings of your thoughts and fancies, boyish sometimes, for you were young still, but in my heart there was an ever-growing tenderness and care for you, which could find no flaw, and feel no weariness. You were apt to be unmindful of the hours, and it was I who made it my duty to watch their flight for you, and see to it that the prayer-bell, the single bell that hung under a little pent-roof against the church, should be tolled at the due time; for Mr. Vernon, in consideration of our heathenish condition, made it a point that the evening service should be read three times a week. And as it was needful that our household should set a pattern to the rest of the villagers, and it interfered with my father's evening pipe, and my mother could not be troubled to change her afternoon cap for her church bonnet, it always fell to my lot to walk with you—do you remember?—only a few hundred yards or so along the brow of the hill, to the little church.

I was about to say that it was the happiest time of my life; but all true life is gain; and the sorrows that befal us are none other than solemn massive foundation-stones laid low in unfathomable gloom, that a measureless content may be built upon them. You remember the first burial-service you had to read, when you besought me to stand beside you at the open grave, because never before had the mournful words been uttered by your lips. It was only the funeral of a little child, and the tiny grave, when the clods were heaped upon it, was no larger than a molehill in the meadows; yet your voice faltered, and your hands trembled as you cast this first small seed into that God's Acre of ours. The autumn night set in while we lingered in silence beside the nameless coffin, long after the mother and her companion who had brought it to its solitary grave, had turned away homeward. It was the flapping of wings close beside us that caused us to lift up our eyes, and from the fir-trees above us four rooks flew home across the darkening sky to their nests in the plain below. You know how of old the flight of birds would fill me with vague superstitions, and just then the heavy fluttering of their dusky wings overhead, as they beat the air for their start, caused a sudden tremor and shudder to thrill through me.

"What ails you, Jane?" you asked.

"Nothing ails me, Mr. Scott," I said.

"Call me Owen," you answered, laying your hand upon my arm, and looking straight into my eyes, for we were of the same height, and stood level with one another: "I do not like to hear you call me anything but Owen. Have you forgotten how we used to play together? Do you remember how I fell into the sheep-pool when we were alone in the valley, and you wasted no time in fruitless cries, but waded in at once, and dragged me out of the water? You would carry me home in your strong arms, though the path was along the hill-side, and you had to rest every few minutes; while I looked up into your rosy face with a very peaceful feeling. Your face is not rosy now, Jane."

How could it be, while your words brought such a dull heavy pain to my heart? I seemed suddenly to be so many, many years older than you! Sometimes of late I had detected myself reckoning your age and mine by the month, and the day of the month, and always finding, with a pang faint and slight, that you were indeed so many years younger than I. Yet the heart takes little heed of age. And I, for the quiet life I had led among the mountains, just one regular single round of summer and winter, coming stealthily and uncounted in their turn from season to season, might have been little more than some yearling creature, that has seen but one spring-time and felt the frosts of but one Christmas. While you, with your great acquirements of learning, and the weighty thoughts that had already wrinkled your broad forehead, and the burden of study that had bowed down your young shoulders, seemed to have borne the full yoke of the years which had laid so gentle a touch upon me.

"I remember very well, Owen," I said; "I was proud of having you to take charge of. But you must go in now; the fog is rising, and you are not over strong."

I spoke with the old tone of authority, and you left me, standing alone beside the little grave. The churchyard extended to the very edge of the steep hill, which looked far and wide over the great plain. It was hidden now by a white lake of mist floating beneath me, upon which the hunting-moon, rising slowly behind the eastern hills, shone down with cold pale beams; for the harvest was over, and the heavy October fogs gathered in the valleys, and hung in light clouds about the fading coppices in the hollows of the mountains. I turned heart-sick to the little open grave, the first in the new graveyard, which was waiting until the sheep were herded for the sexton to fill it up for ever with the clods; the baby hands and feet folded there in eternal rest, had never been stained with selfishness, and the baby lips, sealed in eternal silence, had uttered never a word of bitterness. So, I said, looking down sadly into the narrow tiny grave, so shall it be with my love; I bury it here while it is yet pure and unselfish, like a seed sown in God's Acre; and from it shall spring a plentiful harvest of happiness for Owen, and of great peace for myself.

It may be that the autumn fog was more harmful than usual, for I was ill after that night with my first serious illness; not merely ailing, but hanging doubtfully between life and death. I grew to think of our summer months together as of a time long since passed, and almost enwrapped in forgetfulness. My mother laughed when I stroked her grey hair with my feeble fingers, and told her I felt older than she was.

"Nay," she said, "we must have you younger and bonnier than ever, Jane. We must see what we can do for you before you come down stairs, and meet Owen. Poor Owen! Who would have dreamt that he could be more heart-broken and disconsolate than Jane's own mother? Poor Owen!"

My mother was smiling significantly, and looking keenly at me over her glasses, but I said nothing; only turned away my face from her scrutiny to the frosted window, where winter had traced its delicate patterns upon the lattice panes.

"Jane," she went on, clasping my fingers in hers, "don't you know that we all wish it, Owen's father, and yours, and me? We thought of it before he came here. Owen is poor, but we have enough for both of you, and I love him like my own son. You need never leave the old home. Jane, don't you love Owen?"

"But I am older than he is," I whispered.

"A marvellous difference," she said, with another laugh; "so am I older than father, but who could tell it was so now? And what does it matter if Owen loves you?"

I wish to cast no blame on you, but there was much in your conduct to feed the sweet delusion which brought fresh health and strength to me. You called my mother, "Mother." You sent fond messages by her, which lost nothing in tone or glance by her delighted repetition of them. You considered no walk too far to get flowers for me from the gardens in the plain below. When I grew well enough to come down stairs you received me with a rapture of congratulation. You urged that the blue parlour, with its southern aspect and closely-fitting wainscot, was the warmest room in the house, and you would not be satisfied until the great chintz-covered sofa with its soft cushions was lifted out of its corner, and planted upon the hearth, for me to lie there, watching you while you were busy among your books; and many times a day you read some sentence aloud, or brought a volume to my side that I might look over the same page, while you waited patiently as my slower eyes and brain were longer than yours in taking in the sense. Even when you were away at the rectory—for during my illness you had begun to spend your evenings there, when you had no church duty—I sat in your study, with your books about me, in which there were passages marked out for me to read. I lingered over getting well.

I was lying on the sofa one evening, wrapped in my mother's white shawl, and just passing into a dreamy slumber, when I heard you entering from one of your visits to the rectory. I cannot tell why I did not rouse myself, unless it seemed to me only as part of a dream, but you crossed the floor noiselessly, and stood beside me for a minute or two, looking down—I felt it—upon my changed face, and closed eyelids. Had I been asleep I should never have felt the light, timid, fluttering touch of your lips upon mine. But my eyes opened at once, and you fell back.

"What is it, Owen?" I asked you calmly, for I felt as if by instinct that the caress was not for me. "Why did you kiss me, Owen?"

"I wonder I never did it before," you said, "you are so like a sister to me. I have no other sister, Jane, and my mother died when I was very young."

You stood opposite to me in the bright firelight with a face changing and flushing like a girl's, and a happy youthful buoyant gladness in it very different to your usually quiet aspect. As I looked at you the old pain returned like a forgotten burden upon my heart.

"I am so happy," you said, crossing over the hearth again, and kneeling down beside me.

"Is it anything you can tell me, dear Owen?" I said, laying my hand upon your hair, and wondering even then at the whiteness and thinness of my poor fingers. The door behind you was opened quietly, but you did not hear it, and my mother stood for an instant in the doorway smiling on us both; I felt keenly how she would misunderstand.

Then you spoke to me, shyly at first, but gathering confidence, of Adelaide Vernon. I knew her well: a little lovely graceful creature, with coquettish school-girl ways, which displayed themselves even at church, though her black browed and swarthy aunt sat beside her in the rector's pew. While you spoke, growing eloquent with a lover's rhapsodies, the fair young face, with its pink and white tints, and soft dainty beauty, rose up before me; and your praises seemed to flood my aching heart like a wide breaking in of water, which rolled desolately against me.

I need not remind you of the opposition your love met. Mr. Vernon was averse to marrying his portionless niece to his poor curate of Ratlinghope; but his disapproval was nothing to the vehement rage with which Mrs. Vernon had other views for Adelaide, set her face against it. The rector came up to our house, and told us—you remember?—with tears wrung from him, proud and reticent man as he was, that he dreaded nothing less than a return of that fearful malady of madness, which had kept his wife a prisoner for years under his own roof. There was as bitter, but a more concealed resentment in our own household, which you only felt indirectly and vaguely. I learned now with what a long premeditated plan your father and mine had schemed for our marriage. Your poor foolish love seemed to every one but yourself and me a rash selfishness. Even I thought at times that half Adelaide's love for you sprang from pure contrariness and childish romance, just feeding upon the opposition it met with. How I smoothed your path for you; how, without suffering the coldness of disappointment to creep over me, I sought your happiness in your own way as if it had been mine also; you partly know. So we prevailed at last.

In spite of all my smothered pain, it was pleasant to see you watch the building of your little parsonage, the square red brick house beside the church, with the doors and windows pricked out with blue tesselated tile-work. It was not a stone's throw from our home, and the blue parlour saw little of your presence, and the dust gathered on the books you had been wont to read. But you would have me to share your exultation. Whenever the large beams were being fitted into your roof, or the cope-stones built into your walls, or the blue tiles set round your windows, I must look on with you, and hearken to your fears lest the home should be unworthy of Adelaide. All my sad thoughts—fer day after day you were setting your foot upon my heart—I worked away in busy labour at your house, and in wistful contrivances to make the little nest look elegant and pretty in the sight of Adelaide Vernon.

Your marriage was to be on the Tuesday, and on the Monday I went down with you to the rectory. The place had become familiar to you, all but the long low southern wing, with its blank walls ivy-grown, and with its windows opening upon the other side over a wide shallow mere, fed with the waters of a hundred mountain brooks. They were Mrs. Vernon's apartments, built for her during her protracted and seemingly hopeless malady, for her husband had promised her that she should never be removed from under his roof. She kept them under her own charge, rarely suffering any foot to enter them, and Mr. Vernon drew me aside when we reached the house, and implored me to venture upon making my way, if possible, to his wife, who had shut herself up in them since the previous evening, and had refused to admit even him. I crossed the long narrow passage which separated them from the rest of the dwelling, and rapped gently at the door, and after a minute's silence I heard Mrs. Vernon's voice asking, "Who is there?"

"Only Jane Meadows," I answered.

I was a favourite with her, and after a slight hesitation, the door was opened, and Mrs. Vernon stood before me: her tall and powerful figure wrapped in a dressing-gown, which left the sinewy arms bare to the elbow, while the thick locks of her black hair, just streaked with grey, fell dishevelled about her swarthy face. The room behind her was littered from end to end, and the fire at which she had been sitting was choked up with cinders, while the window, tarnished with dust, gave no glimpse of the mountain landscape beyond. She returned to her chair before the fire, and surveyed me with a sullen frown from under her reddened eyelids. The trembling of her limbs, muscular as they were, and the glistening of her face, told me not more surely than the faint and sickly odour pervading the room, that she had been taking opium.

"Jane," she cried, with a burst of maudlin tears, which she did not attempt to conceal, "come here, and sit down beside me. I am so miserable, Jane. Your mother was here on Saturday, telling me that you love Owen Scott, and everybody wanted him to marry you. Adelaide, the poor little painted doll, is not fit to be his wife, and she will make him wretched. And you will be miserable, like all of us."

My heart sank at the thought of your wretchedness. "I am not miserable," I replied, throwing my own arms round her, and looking up into her wrathful eyes. "You don't know how strong and peaceful we grow when we seek the happiness of those we love. We cannot decide who shall love whom, and it was not God's will that Owen should choose me. Let us make them as happy as we can."

She let me lead her to her seat, and talk to her about you and Adelaide in a way that tranquillised her, until she consented to dress herself with my aid, and return with me to the company assembled in the other part of the house.

But there was something in Adelaide's whole conduct which tended to irritate Mrs. Vernon. She was playing silly pranks upon us all, but especially upon her gloomy aunt, about whom she hovered with a fretting waywardness mingled with an unquiet tenderness, which displayed itself in numberless childish ways; but with such grace and prettiness, that none of us could find it in our hearts to chide her, except Mrs. Vernon herself. I was glad when the time came for us to leave; though you loitered across the lawn, looking back every minute at Adelaide, who stood in the portico: her white dress gleaming amid the shadows, and she kissing her little hand to you with a laugh whose faint musical ringing just reached our ears.

You slept that night, as we often sleep, unwitting that those who are dear to us as our own souls are passing through great perils. You slept, and it was I who watched all night, and called you early in the morning, with the news that the sun was rising over the hills into a cloudless sky, and that your marriage-day was come.

We were at the rectory betimes, yet the villagers had reared an arch of flowers over the gates. Mrs. Vernon, dressed with unusual richness and care, was watching for us at the portico, and received us both with a grave but kindly greeting. All the house was astir with the hurrying of many feet, and the sharp click of doors slamming to and fro; but though you waited restlessly, no one else came near us in the little room where we three sat together, until the door was slowly opened —you turning to it with rapturous impatience —and Mr. Vernon entered and told us that Adelaide was nowhere to be found.

"Don't alarm yourself," said Mr. Vernon to his wife, "but Adelaide has been missing since daybreak; she was gone when her companions went to call her. You remember she used to walk in her sleep if she were much excited; and this morning the hall door was open, and her bonnet was found on the way to Ratlinghope. The agitation of yesterday must have caused this."

"She was coming to me!" you said, with a vivid smile and a glow which faded as you began to realise the fact of Adelaide's disappearance.

The hills stretched away for many a mile, with shelving rocks here and there, which hung over deep still tarns, black with shadows, and hedged in by reedy thickets. And there were narrow rifts, cleaving far down into the living stone of the mountain range, and overgrown with brambles, where the shepherds sometimes heard their lambs bleating piteously, out of sight or reach of help, until the dreary moan died away from the careless echoes. "Children have been lost there," cried Mrs. Vernon, wringing her hands distractedly; and if Adelaide had wandered away in the darkness, she might be lying now dead in the depths of the black tarns, or imprisoned alive in one of the clefts of the rocks.

I never left your side that day; and as hour after hour passed by, I saw a grey ghastly change creep over your young face, as your heart died within you. Mrs. Vernon kept close beside us, though we soon distanced every other seeker, and her wonderful strength continued unabated, even when your despairing energy was exhausted. I knew the mountains as well as the shepherds did; and from one black unruffled tarn, to another like itself, gloomy and secret-looking, I led you without speaking; save that into every gorge, whose depth our straining eyes could not penetrate, we called aloud, until the dark dank walls of the gulf muttered back the name of Adelaide. There was no foot-weariness for us as long as the daylight lasted; and it seemed as if the sun *could* not go down until we had found her. Now and then we tarried upon the brow of some headland, with our hands lifted to our ears that we might catch the most distant whisper of the signal-bells; the faintest tone that ever reached the uplands, if there were any to be borne to us upon the breeze, from the church belfry in the plain far away.

The search was continued for many days; but

no trace of Adelaide was found, except a lace cap which lay soiled and wet with dew near to one of the tarns which we three had visited; but without discovering it then. Mrs. Vernon rallied our hopes and energies long after all reasonable ground for either was lost, and then she fell into a depression of spirits which almost threatened a renewal of her early malady. She collected all Adelaide's little possessions, and spent many hours of each day among them in her own apartments; but she was always ready to leave them, when you, in your sore grief, wandered to the old home of the lost girl; and then she strove to console you with a patient tenderness strange to see in a woman so rigid and haughty. But you refused to be comforted; and putting on one side all the duties of your office, you roamed ceaselessly about the hills; dragging yourself back again almost lifeless to our house—for your own you would never enter—and asking me night after night, as the sunset and darkness spread upon the mountains, if there were no place left unexplored. As though it were possible to call back again the dead past, and find her yet alive among the desolate hills!

In the midst of it all another trouble befel us. Before the new year came in, my mother fell ill of the sickness in which she died. I think that first roused you from the solitude of your despair. Though you could not yet front the kindly familiar faces of your old congregation, there seemed to be some little break in the cloud of hopelessness which hung about you, in the care you began to feel for her. It was but a few days before she died, and after you had been reading to her, as she lay very feeble, and often dozing away with weakness, that she suddenly roused herself, and looked at you with eager, eyes.

"You'll always be fond of Jane, Owen?"

"Always. She has been the truest of sisters to me."

"Ah!" sighed my mother, "you little think how she has loved you. Not one woman in a thousand could have done as our Jane has. Boy, it's not possible you'll ever be loved so again on earth."

You had never thought of it before, and your face grew paler than my mother's. I sat behind the curtains, where you could see me though she could not; and you looked across at me fixedly, still keeping your station by her side. I smiled with the tears standing in my eyes, but with no foolish burning in my cheeks, for if it would comfort you in any degree, I was neither afraid nor ashamed that you should know it.

"Ever since you came," my mother murmured, "smoothing every stone out of your path, and only fretting because she could not bear every trouble for you! If you ever marry, Owen, she will live only for you, and your wife and children. You will always care for her, Owen?"

"I will never marry any other woman," you said, laying your lips upon my mother's wrinkled hand.

I know it was a comfort to you. Perhaps in the suddenness and mystery of your loss, you felt as if everything was wrecked, and nothing remained to life but a bleak, black dreariness.

But from that hour, there was a light, very feeble and dim and lustreless—a mere glow-worm in the waste wilderness—which shone upon your path. You began to return to your old duties, though it was as if you were leaning upon me, and trusting to my guiding. There was no talk of love between us; it was enough that we understood one another.

We might have gone on quietly thus, year after year, until the memory of Adelaide had faded away, but that it was not many months before my father, who had been younger than my mother, and was a fine man yet, announced to me that he was about to marry again. The news had reached you elsewhere; for, on the same evening, while I was sitting alone with my troubled thoughts, you called me into the blue parlour, and made me take my old seat in the corner of the chintz-covered sofa, while you knelt down beside me.

"Jane," you said, very gently, "I want to offer my poor home to you."

"No, no, Owen," I cried, looking down upon your face, so grey and unsmiling, with dark circles under your sunken eyes, "you are young yet, and will meet with some other woman—a dear sister she shall ever be to me—younger and brighter, and more fitted for you than I am. You shall not sacrifice yourself to me."

"But, Jane," you urged, and a pleasant light dawned in your eyes, "I cannot do without you. You know I could not go alone into yonder little house, which stands empty by the church; and how could I go away from Ratlinghope, leaving you behind me? I have no home but where you are; and I love you more than I ever thought to love any woman again."

Maybe you remember what more you said; every word is in my heart to this day.

I thought it over in the quiet night. You were poor, and I, inheriting my mother's fortune, could surround you with comforts; secretly in my judgment, there had grown the conviction that you would never be what the world calls a prosperous man. The time was come when we must be separated or united for ever; and if you parted from me, I could never more stand between you and any sorrow. So I became your wife nearly twelve months after your great loss and misery.

Those first weeks of our marriage had more sunshine than I had ever dared to hope for. You seemed to shake off a great burden, now that it was irrevocably settled that our lives were to be passed together. Not a single lurking dread remained in my heart that you were otherwise than happy.

We came back to England some days earlier than we intended, for a letter reached me after many delays, with the news that Mrs. Vernon was ill, and implored us to hasten our return. We stayed on our way homeward at the rectory, where I soon left you with Mr. Vernon, while I was conducted to the entrance of the long passage which led to Mrs. Vernon's apartments. Her lady, the servant said in a whisper, was ailing more in mind than in body, and she dared not disobey her strict orders not to venture further. I went on, for I knew her caprices; and once again I was admitted, when she heard me say, calling myself by your name, that it was Jane Scott who sought entrance. There was no new gleam of madness in her dark eyes. She grasped my hands nervously, and held them fast, while she questioned me about our journey, and what your manner had been. Were you happy? Had you altogether ceased to grieve for Adelaide? Was your whole love mine? Was there perfect unalloyed content in our mutual affection?

"Jane," she said, with her lips close to my ear, though she spoke in a loud shrill tone, "I had sworn that Adelaide should never marry Owen Scott. Partly for your sake, for your mother said it was killing you. Partly because it was better for her to marry my rich nephew. Jane, I must have what I set my mind upon, or I should die. What was Adelaide, that I should lose my life, or worse, ten times worse, lose my reason again for her sake? I did it for the best, Jane. I never thought how it was to end. It only seemed to me, if I could hide her from one day till the next, something would happen. But it was a long long time, a dreadful time, till Owen came to tell us he was going to marry you. You understand, Jane?"

"No, no!" I cried.

"It seemed so easy a thing to do, and best for all of us. I carried her here in the night, like the baby she is. I have never been cruel to her, never, Jane. But the time seemed long, long, and she was wild and cunning at first. I only thought of a little while, and afterwards I grew afraid. But she will not come out now, though I try to rouse her. Go in, Jane, and make her come out!"

Mrs. Vernon drew me across the inner apartment to the door of a small chamber, padded throughout, and with no opening except into the ante-room. It had been constructed for herself in the seasons of her most dangerous paroxysms, and was so carefully planned that no sound of her wild ravings could be heard, and no glimpse of her face could be seen, through the window which overlooked the mere. And here lay your Adelaide asleep, wan and emaciated, with a dimness on her golden curls, and all the rosy tints of her beauty faded.

"She has been taking laudanum," said Mrs. Vernon. "I gave it to her at first, when I was compelled to be away for a long time, and now she has a craving for it. I have never been cruel to her, Jane. She has had everything she wanted."

You know how I came down to the library, where you and Mr. Vernon were sitting, and told you and Mr. Vernon all. You know how, while Mr. Vernon bowed his grey head upon his hands, you stretched out your arms to me, and cried, with an exceeding bitter cry as if I could find a remedy for you, "Help me, Jane!"

Dear, my heart fluttered towards you for a moment, longing to be clasped in your outstretched arms, and pour out all my love to you, which had ever been tongue-tied, lest you should weary of it; but I hardened myself against the yearning. In the great mirror on the staircase I scarcely knew the white-faced despairing woman, who was sweeping by, erect and stern, and the two men with downcast heads and lingering footsteps who were following her. You spoke no word, either of you, but passed through the outer apartment, with its tarnished window and sullied disorder, where Mrs. Vernon sat cowering in the furthest corner, and entered the room within, where Adelaide lay asleep, but breathing fitfully, as on the verge of waking. I dragged myself (for I was faint) to the casement, which I pushed open, and looked out upon the purple hills, purple with heather-bells, where we had thought her unknown tomb was. Up yonder stood our home, the home we had built for Adelaide, and which we had never yet entered; and turning away my aching eyes from it, I looked back again upon you, who were standing beside her, with a depth of tender and horror-stricken pity on your bending face.

Whether it was the fresh air from the hills, or some mysterious influence of your presence penetrating her sleeping senses, we cannot tell; but while I looked, unable to turn away my eyes from you both, her mouth quivered, and her long eyelashes trembled, half opening and closing again, as if too languid to bear the light, until you touched her hands softly and timidly, and breathed "Adelaide!" And she awoke fully, with a sharp shrill cry, as if you were at last come for her deliverance, and springing into your arms, she clung to you, with her little hands clasped round you as though they would never unlock again; while you laid your cheek down upon her dim dishevelled curls, and I heard you murmur, "My darling!" Yet yonder was our home, yours and mine, Owen; and the ring that was on my finger—the only one I wore, I cared so much for it—was our marriage-ring.

You turned to me, Owen, with that full, searching gaze, eye to eye, and soul to soul, which we could bear from one another. Adelaide was come back from the dead to bring to us greater sorrow than her death had brought. We saw it all, you and I, while she was still clinging to you with sobs and childish caresses, and I stood aloof at the window. I knew how much you had to say to her which no other ear might listen to. I knew what it would be wisest and best to do. I took Mr. Vernon's arm, and I drew him away from the room, and I left you and Adelaide together.

I know now that it was not long before you came to me—only ten minutes—such a trifle of time as one gives ungrudgingly to the dreariest beggar on the roadside who has a piteous tale to tell. But all the past, and all the dreaded future being present with me, the moments seemed endless in their immortal bitterness, until you entered the room where I had shut myself in alone, and coming swiftly up to me where I stood upon the hearth, hid your face upon my shoulder with strong sobs and tears.

"I will go away, Jane," you said at last, "by myself for a few days, till she is gone from here.

You will take care of her for me. She knows all now."

"I will do anything for you," I answered, still chary of my words, as it was my wont to be, lest my love should weary you.

You left me, as it was best you should do, alone, with the charge of that perplexed household upon me; Adelaide broken in health and spirits; Mrs. Vernon plunged into the frenzy of her old malady; the story running far and wide throughout the country. Every day I found my comfort and strength in the letter that came from you, wherein you had the generosity to lay bare your heart to me as frankly as ever. So the hard task began to grow lighter; the tangled coil to unravel itself. Mr. Vernon procured a nurse to take care of his wife, and I accompanied Adelaide to the distant dwelling of some friends, where we hoped she might sooner recover her health; nor did I leave her until I saw her resuming her playful girlish ways, and coquettish graces. At last I was free to go home; to go to the home you and I had built on the rock, watching together its beams laid, and its roof raised. But I was alone there. If Adelaide had been your young and beautiful wife, you would have crossed the threshold hand in hand, uttering such words of welcome as would never have died out of her memory, if it had been like mine.

The jealous misgiving was unworthy of you and myself, dear. I paced the little rooms, taking up the trinkets which you had bought anxiously and lavishly for Adelaide, and always laying them down again with a sharper pang. Did you wish me to die, Owen? Was your heart aching to take her back again? I rested at last in your little study, where your books lay in scattered heaps before the empty shelves. The days were gone for ever when we had read them together on the hillside, in the first careless freedom of your sojourn with us. I sat down among them, covering my face with my hands, and I heard and I saw nothing.

Nothing, my love, my dear, until your hand rested on my head, and your voice, in hearty cheery tones, fell on my delighted ear.

"Jane," you said, "my darling, my wife! We are come home at last. I meant to be here first, but it is ever you who welcome me. The trouble is past. I love you better, love you more, than ever I loved Adelaide."

You lifted up my head, and made me look into your face. It was at once peaceful and exultant, as the face of a man who has gone through a great conflict, and come out of it more than conqueror. You laid your lips to mine with one long kiss, which told me infinitely better than words could tell, that never more need shadow of doubt or distrust of your love fall upon my spirit. Such as I was, you gathered me into your inmost heart, barring it against any memory or any fancy that might betray me. The deep foundations had been laid, and any storm that beat against our confidence and content would beat against them all in vain.

Love, we have learned to speak of the past calmly, and Adelaide has been to see us with her husband.

VII.

MRS. LIRRIPER RELATES
HOW JEMMY TOPPED UP.

Well my dear and so the evening readings of these jottings of the Major's brought us round at last to the evening when we were all packed and going away next day, and I do assure you that by that time though it was deliciously comfortable to look forward to the dear old house in Norfolk-street again, I had formed quite a high opinion of the French nation and had noticed them to be much more homely and domestic in their families and far more simple and amiable in their lives than I had ever been led to expect, and it did strike me between ourselves that in one particular they might be imitated to advantage by another nation which I will not mention, and that is in the courage with which they take their little enjoyments on little means and with little things and don't let solemn big-wigs stare them out of countenance or speechify them dull, of which said solemn big-wigs I have ever had the one opinion that I wish they were all made comfortable separately in coppers with the lids on and never let out any more.

"Now young man," I says to Jemmy when we brought our chairs into the balcony that last evening, "you please to remember who was to 'top up.'"

"All right Gran" says Jemmy. "I am the illustrious personage."

But he looked so serious after he had made me that light answer, that the Major raised his eyebrows at me and I raised mine at the Major.

"Gran and Godfather," says Jemmy, "you can hardly think how much my mind has run on Mr. Edson's death."

It gave me a little check. "Ah! It was a sad scene my love" I says, "and sad remembrances come back stronger than merry. But this" I says after a little silence, to rouse myself and the Major and Jemmy all together, "is not topping up. Tell us your story my dear."

"I will" says Jemmy.

"What is the date sir?" says I. "Once upon a time when pigs drank wine?"

"No Gran," says Jemmy, still serious; "once upon a time when the French drank wine."

Again I glanced at the Major, and the Major glanced at me.

"In short, Gran and Godfather," says Jemmy, looking up, "the date is this time, and I'm going to tell you Mr. Edson's story."

The flutter that it threw me into. The change of colour on the part of the Major!

"That is to say, you understand," our bright-eyed boy says, "I am going to give you my version of it. I shall not ask whether it's right or not, firstly because you said you knew very little about it, Gran, and secondly because what little you did know was a secret."

I folded my hands in my lap and I never took my eyes off Jemmy as he went running on.

"The unfortunate gentleman" Jemmy commences, "who is the subject of our present narrative was the son of Somebody, and was born Somewhere, and chose a profession Somehow. It is not with those parts of his career that we have to deal; but with his early attachment to a young and beautiful lady."

I thought I should have dropped. I durstn't look at the Major; but I knew what his state was, without looking at him.

"The father of our ill-starred hero" says Jemmy, copying as it seemed to me the style of some of his story-books, "was a worldly man who entertained ambitious views for his only son and who firmly set his face against the contemplated alliance with a virtuous but penniless orphan. Indeed he went so far as roundly to assure our hero that unless he weaned his thoughts from the object of his devoted affection, he would disinherit him. At the same time, he proposed as a suitable match, the daughter of a neighbouring gentleman of a good estate, who was neither ill favoured nor unamiable, and whose eligibility in a pecuniary point of view could not be disputed. But young Mr. Edson, true to the first and only love that had inflamed his breast, rejected all considerations of self-advancement, and, deprecating his father's anger in a respectful letter, ran away with her."

My dear I had begun to take a turn for the better, but when it come to running away I began to take another turn for the worse.

"The lovers" says Jemmy "fled to London and were united at the altar of Saint Clement's Danes. And it is at this period of their simple but touching story, that we find them inmates of the dwelling of a highly respected and beloved lady of the name of Gran, residing within a hundred miles of Norfolk-street."

I felt that we were almost safe now, I felt that the dear boy had no suspicion of the bitter truth, and I looked at the Major for the first time and drew a long breath. The Major gave me a nod.

"Our hero's father" Jemmy goes on "proving implacable and carrying his threat into unrelenting execution, the struggles of the young couple in London were severe, and would have been far more so, but for their good angel's having conducted them to the abode of Mrs. Gran: who, divining their poverty (in spite of their endeavours to conceal it from her), by a thousand delicate arts smoothed their rough way, and alleviated the sharpness of their first distress."

Here Jemmy took one of my hands in one of his, and began a marking the turns of his story by making me give a beat from time to time upon his other hand.

"After a while, they left the house of Mrs. Gran, and pursued their fortunes through a variety of successes and failures elsewhere. But in all reverses, whether for good or evil, the words of Mr. Edson to the fair young partner of his life, were: 'Unchanging Love and Truth will carry us through all!'"

My hand trembled in the dear boy's, those words were so wofully unlike the fact.

"Unchanging Love and Truth" says Jemmy over again, as if he had a proud kind of a noble pleasure in it, "will carry us through all! Those were his words. And so they fought their way, poor but gallant and happy, until Mrs. Edson gave birth to a child."

"A daughter," I says.

"No" says Jemmy, "a son. And the father was so proud of it that he could hardly bear it out of his sight. But a dark cloud overspread the scene. Mrs. Edson sickened, drooped, and died."

"Ah! Sickened, drooped, and died!" I says.

"And so Mr. Edson's only comfort, only hope on earth, and only stimulus to action, was his darling boy. As the child grew older, he grew so like his mother that he was her living picture. It used to make him wonder why his father cried when he kissed him. But unhappily he was like his mother in constitution as well as in face, and he died too before he had grown out of childhood. Then Mr. Edson, who had good abilities, in his forlornness and despair threw them all to the winds. He became apathetic, reckless, lost. Little by little he sank down, down, down, down, until at last he almost lived (I think) by gaming. And so sickness overtook him in the town of Sens in France, and he lay down to die. But now that he laid him down when all was done, and looked back upon the green Past beyond the time when he had covered it with ashes, he thought gratefully of the good Mrs. Gran long lost sight of, who had been so kind to him and his young wife in the early days of their marriage, and he left the little that he had as a last Legacy to her. And she, being brought to see him, at first no more knew him than she would know from seeing the ruin of a Greek or Roman Temple, what it used to be before it fell; but at length she remembered him. And then he told her with tears, of his regret for the misspent part of his life, and besought her to think as mildly of it as she could, because it was the poor fallen Angel of his unchanging Love and Constancy after all. And because she had her grandson with her, and he fancied that his own boy, if he had lived, might have grown to be something like him, he asked her to let him touch his forehead with his cheek and say certain parting words."

Jemmy's voice sank low when it got to that, and tears filled my eyes, and filled the Major's.

"You little Conjuror" I says, "how did you ever make it all out? Go in and write it every word down, for it's a wonder."

Which Jemmy did, and I have repeated it to you my dear from his writing.

Then the Major took my hand and kissed it, and said "Dearest madam all has prospered with us."

"Ah Major" I says drying my eyes, "we needn't have been afraid. We might have known it. Treachery don't come natural to beaming youth; but trust and pity, love and constancy—they do, thank God!"

THE END OF THE CHRISTMAS NUMBER FOR 1864.

The right of Translating any portion of MRS. LIRRIPER'S LEGACY *is reserved by the Authors.*

Published at the Office, No. 26, Wellington Street, Strand. Printed by C. WHITING, Beaufort House, Strand.

www.ingramcontent.com/pod-product-compliance
Lightning Source LLC
Chambersburg PA
CBHW022157020726
47496CB00008B/2754